THE SEA OF ALWAYS

Also by Jodi Lynn Anderson

The Thirteen Witches series
The Memory Thief

My Diary from the Edge of the World

The May Bird trilogy
The Ever After
Among the Stars
Warrior Princess

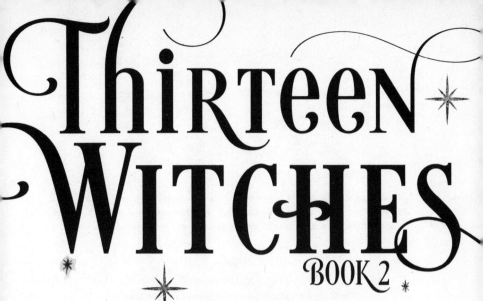

Thirteen Witches

Book 2

The Sea of Always

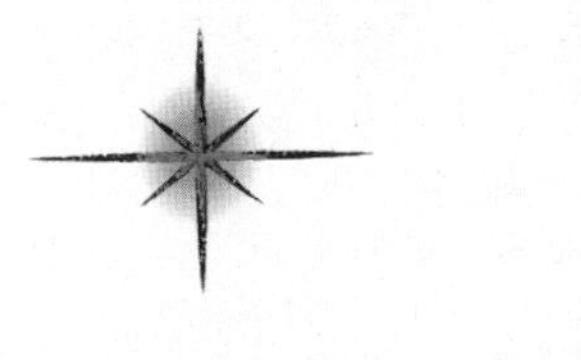

Jodi Lynn Anderson

Aladdin

New York London Toronto Sydney New Delhi

This book is a work of fiction. Any references to historical events, real people, or real places are used fictitiously. Other names, characters, places, and events are products of the author's imagination, and any resemblance to actual events or places or persons, living or dead, is entirely coincidental.

ALADDIN
An imprint of Simon & Schuster Children's Publishing Division
1230 Avenue of the Americas, New York, New York 10020
First Aladdin hardcover edition April 2022

Designed by Heather Palisi
The text of this book was set in Adobe Caslon Pro.
Manufactured in the United States of America 0222 FFG
2 4 6 8 10 9 7 5 3 1
CIP data for this book is available from the Library of Congress.
ISBN 9781481480246 (hc)
ISBN 9781481480260 (ebook)

For Tina—a bright light

You are the cloud-builder; you are the grower of wings. You are the one whom Earth entrusts its stories to; you are the singer of songs. Reader, look behind you. You have left moonlight where you've walked, though you may not remember it.

—*Inscription from a cross-stitched pillow in the Brightweaver's cottage*

THE SEA OF ALWAYS

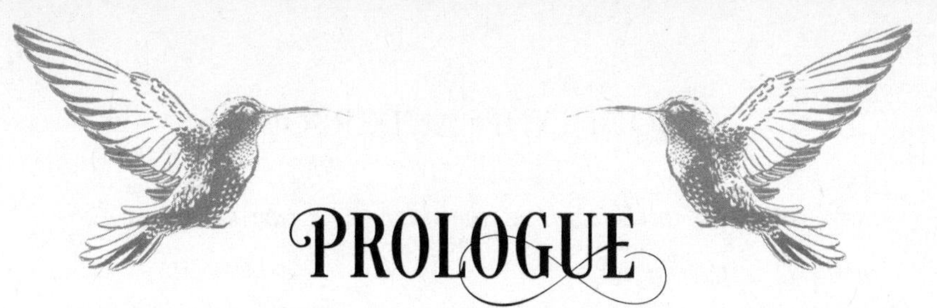

PROLOGUE

In the middle of the night, in a house at the end of Waterside Road, two women sit by a window looking out at the sea. They lean toward each other in their chairs as if closeness will protect them from something they fear. Outside, the frigid wind blows at the glass. It is dark moon, and Annabelle Oaks has an uneasy feeling that something is coming.

On her left, Elaine Bartley is wearing a sweatshirt that says I Could Be Wrong but Probably Not *in faded puffed letters. She's flipping through the pages of a mystery novel but barely reading it. Annabelle is elegant in a tiered cotton dress, and smudged with paint as she stares at a canvas she is dabbing at with a brush.*

They're unlikely companions, and yet the months since their daughters left have brought them together evening after evening, in this ritual of watching and waiting. On a table between them, a piece of paper lies open. It's never far from Annabelle even when she sleeps. It's the note their daughters left behind the night they went away:

I'm going to find him, *it reads. And then, below that, in a postscript scribbled crookedly at the bottom:*

I'm going too.

The first sentence is neat and steady, as if the few words it contains were measured out carefully by its author. The second sentence is sloped and wild, as if one girl were catching up to the other on her way out the door . . . as if it were written at a sprint.

This is the note the women showed the police—who believe the girls have run away to track down lost fathers they will never find. Annabelle, of course, knows better.

A sailor in a yellow rain slicker drifts into the room and then right through Elaine, to get to the kitchen. Elaine sits up taller, shivering.

"That's Soggy that went through you," Annabelle says. "Sorry. He's really quite distracted since losing Crafty Agatha."

Mrs. Bartley shivers again, looking around, then turns back to her book. She doesn't have the sight; she can't see the ghosts milling about the room, but she does sense the cold of them. The room, which would look empty to almost anyone, is actually full of spirits. More and more have come every day since Rosie left, ghosts from nearby towns and counties trying to get a glance at the Oaks family home before drifting back to their graves by morning. The death of the Memory Thief has made this house more infamous than it already was.

Annabelle knows that her companion believes her about all of it: the ghosts, the witches, the Moon Goddess, the war. She knows it's easier to believe in impossible things than to believe that someone you love is truly lost; better to think your daughter is off on a dangerous journey she chose than to believe the alternative. But Annabelle knows, also, that Elaine does not know enough of witches to fear them as she should.

Finally Annabelle's visitor stands up. "Heading home," she says, laying a gentle hand on Annabelle's shoulder before turning and shuffling toward the door. Most nights, she's here until she can barely keep her eyes open. And then she returns with circles under her eyes the next evening.

After she goes, Annabelle turns back to her painting, smudging and dotting the canvas with her brushstrokes, rendering a portrait of her grandmother. As with all her other work, there is something foreboding about it. The things Annabelle renders can't help but take a dark turn: flowers wilt in their vases, faces frown, storms whip forests of trees. There is a warning in her grandmother's eyes.

"They're out there swimming, waiting for me," Annabelle says to no one—to the painting, to the ghosts, the walls, the air, the stars.

In her mind she sees her children: Rosie, short, quirky, strong, and brave; and Wolf, a baby boy she only knew for moments before she was robbed of him. She aches with the memory—now returned to her—of the two of them on the day they were born. The tight, trusting grip of Wolf's tiny hand, the sweet smell of the top of his head, the wide wonder in his eyes looking out at the world. Rosie weeping after he was taken away that morning, reaching for him as if she'd lost her own arms.

One child stolen. The other now grown, and off like a thief in the night with her best friend to save him . . . wherever in time he might be.

It is this that draws Annabelle out of her chair to stare at the sea. They're out there swimming, *she thinks, looking out on the cold dark waves of the Atlantic.* And I can't keep them safe.

✦ ✦ ✦

The lonesome house glows like a beacon through the long night. Annabelle hates when the ghosts leave her alone just before daybreak, and as darkness creeps close to dawn, she watches with regret as they drift into the woods. The yard grows quiet and still. And then . . . she hears it. The rustle through the trees, as if the leaves are whispering about something they are afraid of, before falling utterly silent.

And suddenly Annabelle sees why.

A figure stands at the edge of the yard, where the grass meets the horizon of the sea. Annabelle's hands begin to shake.

The witch standing across her yard doesn't move. She is far enough away that her face is only a white oval in the dim light. Annabelle doesn't recognize her except to know what *she is.*

"Annabelle Oaks," the witch calls across the still air, "your daughter will die."

And it feels like boulders hung around her neck, to hear such a thing.

And then the witch turns and drifts down the trail at the side of the cliff, still moments before the sun can rise. Once she's gone from view, Annabelle sinks to the floor, all the strength leaving her.

She would swim to Rosie if she could.

But no boat, no submarine, could carry her there.

There's only one way to travel through the Sea of Always. And Rosie took that with her.

CHAPTER 1

The problem with living inside the belly of a magical whale for eighty-eight days is the boredom. My best friend, Germ, and I are making the best of it by playing War.

"You got all the aces," Germ says. She is lounging on a La-Z-Boy, eating Doritos. "You always get aces."

"You're exaggerating," I say. But she's right, I do get all the aces.

I look at my hand, the wrinkled cards we've played a thousand times since boarding. My pile is huge and Germ's is dwindling. This happens all the time, and yet . . . and yet . . . somehow, even though it's purely a game of chance, Germ always wins. I'm so close to victory, I can taste it, but I'm pretty sure it will slip away.

I know this is not typically what anyone would expect to find in here, two twelve-year-old girls playing cards and stuffing their faces. To look around, you wouldn't even know we're inside an ageless, time-traveling creature at all. If anything, it looks like Germ's grammie's house, which I visited once when we were little.

Off to the right is our bedroom, with an orange rug and two beds where we sleep. Here in the center there's a TV and two beat-up La-Z-Boys, with bowls full of our favorite snacks on a table in between. There's also a dining table and a shag rug, and a treadmill and mini trampoline for Germ, who can never sit still for long.

Still, there are *some* indicators that we're not in Kansas anymore. For one thing, there's a giant glass "moonroof" above that affords us a view of the blue ocean water above. There are travel brochures littering the room that offer guidance on trips to the Stone Age, the Bronze Age, specific eras like the Han dynasty, the Gupta empire, and so on. There's also a full-color coffee-table book called *Welcome to the Sea of Always* that includes a primer on the magical creatures of the ocean of time, and a terrifying who's who profile on someone called the pirate king and his army of bones. Plus a rundown on the rules of time travel, which includes things like:

> *No crossing paths with your former or future self unless you want to create a troublesome wormhole.*
>
> *People of the past can't see you unless they have the sight.*
>
> *No returning to your starting place until your journey is at an end.*

The book and brochures came in a gift basket that was waiting for us when we boarded—the kind you get from nice hotels, full of colorful tissue paper and apples and pears and a pineapple and some chocolate bars, plus spare toothpaste and some welcome papers. Germ and I long ago devoured the chocolate, tossed the fruit, and made tiny spitballs out of the tissue paper to shoot through straws at each other.

Anyway, we basically have everything two twelve-year-old girls could need while traveling through time—

except our moms, and school, and humans besides each other.

Germ's theory is that the whale (whom she's named Chompy . . . since her favorite name, *Chauncey*, didn't fit right) provides everything you need for whatever kind of passenger you are, hence the Doritos and the Pop-Tarts. (The first three days, I ate Pop-Tarts until I barfed.) It also explains why there are photos of her boyfriend, D'quan Daniels, and Olympic women athletes magically pasted on the wall beside her bed, while on my side there are favorite books of mine like *The Secret Garden* and *One Crazy Summer* and *Because of Winn-Dixie*, and some of my favorites from when I was little, like *The Snowy Day*. It explains why Germ's favorite show, *LA Pet Psychic*, is on permanent loop on the TV and why we have several copies of *Pet Psychic* magazine on the coffee table. There are also cinnamon-scented candles (Germ loves cinnamon-scented candles) and matchbooks everywhere to light them.

We have everything we need. But the truth is, time feels endless inside the whale, and I guess that's because it is. I think it's safe to say that in the outside world (the one we left behind), time is passing . . . but within our whale, time stands still. I know this because I have a tiny hourglass necklace given to me by a witch, and not a grain of sand has dropped through it . . . and yet, according to Germ's watch, eighty-eight days have passed. We keep track of *that time* (home time) by marking the wall with a Sharpie (thanks, Chompy!) every time Germ's watch circles noon. So somehow time is moving, and also it's not.

Either way, we're excruciatingly bored—and so we've passed the days by trying at least fifty ways to wear eyeliner, played at least a thousand games of War, painted our toenails every color of the rainbow, had hour-long burping contests, ranked all the boys at our school back home in terms of cuteness. (Germ is devoted to D'quan but says you can't blame a girl for looking. And anyway, D'quan doesn't know the real reason why we disappeared and might think we're dead.)

We've discussed what seventh grade is going to be like if we live to see some of it, and I have promised to let Germ drag me to more parties, and promised to at least try to like her other bestie, Bibi West (who now prefers to be called by her full name, Bibiana, though we can't get used to it and always forget). We've read all the travel guides Chompy has provided. We've read and reread our most important book of all, *The Witch Hunter's Guide to the Universe*, backward and forward a thousand times. Germ has made me a special friendship bracelet to hold my whale whistle to my wrist. And now . . . we're back to War.

"Aw! Isn't Chompy sweet?" Germ squeals, looking over at a small bowl of M&M's that has appeared beside me. Staring at my M&M's, I bite my tongue. Chompy *does* seem to anticipate all our needs. (He's very subtle about it. You look away for a moment, or blink your eyes, or start to daydream, and that's when he changes things on you.) BUT Chompy also used to serve a witch (granted, the witch is dead) whose whistle now belongs to us.

"He'd probably be just as eager to provide witches whatever *they* needed," I say. "Like, we get M&M's. . . . They get cauldrons for cooking children in."

"Shh. You'll hurt his feelings," Germ hisses, glancing at the domed ceiling above us.

Chompy gives a shudder. Which makes me, for a moment, panicked. I'm always nervous that at any moment something on Chompy could go haywire. In the grand scheme of things, we're a very tiny vessel surrounded by seawater that could drown us, after all.

"See?" Germ says with accusing eyes.

"He was avoiding that octopus," I say, pointing out the moonroof at an enormous red creature floating above and past us.

Germ softens again, and she grins. "Every time I think of octopuses, I think about that time in first grade."

I lay my ace down and swipe Germ's jack, flustered. *Here we go.*

It's one of the infamous moments of my childhood. At school we were playing the Farmer in the Dell, where everyone picks partners until someone is a supposedly lonely, solitary piece of cheese. (Don't ask me, I didn't invent the special brand of torture that is the Farmer in the Dell.)

Someone had already picked Germ, so I knew I would be the cheese at the end, which would be horribly embarrassing. And so when the game was whittled down to about three people, I pointed out the window and yelled that purple eight-armed aliens were invading from outer space and we all needed to run for our lives. Somehow, I was so convincing that I got everyone to look out the window at the sky.

"That was the best," Germ says, ignoring the fact that being the girl who pretended we were being attacked by aliens turned out to be way more embarrassing than being the cheese. She lays down an ace, her only one, and we go to war. She wins with a seven to my five, and gains a bunch of cards. The next round is a war too; Germ wins again. My pile dwindles.

I feel a reluctant smile creep onto my face. Germ seems

to think that all sorts of things about me are charming, things I wish I could change—like how I scowl at people I don't know and spend most of our schooltime looking out the window imagining how nice it would be to walk through a door into the clouds, away from everyone but my best friend.

She lays down a nine that brings us to war. While I've been ruminating on my shortcomings, she's managed to get the last two of my aces. Ugh.

The rest of the game follows suit. Germ's hands move quickly as she confiscates my best cards. Soon they're all gone. She looks at me apologetically.

"Sorry, Rosie, I really wanted you to win."

"That's okay," I say. "I wanted you to win too."

She yawns. "I'm gonna turn in."

Germ goes to our room and shimmies into a hot-pink pajama ensemble, provided by Chompy of course, that sets off her pale pinkish freckled cheeks and strawberry-blond hair and fits her ample frame perfectly. I change into an oversize T-shirt and sloppy flannel pants. Germ brushes her teeth and washes her face with this new cream she's been using. I run a brush over my teeth but skip the washing. Germ says "I look gorgeous" to the mirror and crawls into bed—a waterbed she's always dreamt of having. I glance at my own reflection—unbrushed brown hair, teeth too big for my mouth, shoulders too high for my neck. I've been waiting for a growth spurt all my life, and now that I'm having one, it seems like all my body parts are growing at different rates.

Germ kneels by her bed and does her nightly ritual: a Hail Mary and an Our Father. Then a prayer to the Moon Goddess for good measure. It's not all that conventional for a Catholic to believe in a goddess who lives on the moon, but Germ is her own person.

"Moon Goddess," she says to the ceiling, "please look after Ebb, wherever he is . . . even if he's nothing."

I wince; an ache flares in my chest. The last time we saw our ghost friend Ebb was the night the Time Witch came and did something terrible to him. (We'll probably never know what.) He was already dead when I knew him, but he's probably *worse* than dead now.

"And please," Germ adds, "send someone, preferably an adult, to help us kill the witches." She pops an eye open to glance at me for a second, then closes it again. "Rosie's great and all, and I'm sure she'll nail it," she says unconvincingly, "but come on, some help would be nice. Thank you."

Then she lies down. She lies with her eyes closed, but keeps talking.

"What do you think my mom's doing right now?" she says.

I'm quiet for a moment. "Missing you."

Germ sighs and pauses briefly before continuing.

"Do you think people are sleeping over at Bibi's right now? It might be Friday night. Friday nights are party nights when you get to seventh grade."

"I think party nights are more like when you're in high school," I say, though Bibi does have a lot of sleepovers.

Germ nods, her eyes still closed, a slight frown playing on her lips.

"I don't want to miss seventh grade," she says.

"I know, Germ," I say back.

"But I want to be here too."

"I know."

And despite what we are here for, and where we are going and why we are on this whale at all, Germ falls asleep quickly. She sleeps the sleep of the untroubled and the brave.

I stay awake; I am neither untroubled nor brave. My courage has yet to show up.

You'll have to go through them to get to me. That's what the Time Witch said, the night she came to me. Eleven witches left. And to save Wolf, I am to kill them all. Somehow, beyond all laws of reason, I—homework-forgetting, cloud-watching, non-friend-making Rosie Oaks, the girl who hides in the corner at school dances, *the one who has to be the cheese*—am the world's last and only witch hunter.

I would never tell Germ this, but I know—*know* for certain—I can't do it.

Restless, I walk on soft feet to the front of our ship and tread up the three carpeted steps to the soothing space nestled like a large berth above Chompy's mouth and a few feet above the level of the living room, where his brain would probably be if he weren't a magical creature. This is the strangest and most magical section of our vessel. We call it "the Grand View."

There are two velvet curtains parted to either side, framing a dark, open space with two comfy leather seats facing a concave black wall. Just in front of the wall, on the floor, is a circle glowing with silvery light—like the kind you might see in a pool at night. But unlike pool lights, *this* light is magical, and projects a beam upward and all around us in a kind of sphere that holds luminous, three-dimensional images.

They float and fly around me, representing a 360-degree view of the ocean that surrounds us—blue 3D images of underwater volcanoes, dark sea-floor caves, giant fish, and so on. Right now, aside from the odd giant jellyfish or squid, the glowing space is bluish and blank, showing the ocean around us as mostly empty.

In the very center of the room is the *map*, which floats blue and translucent and flat, as if laid out on an invisible table.

The map itself is really two things overlaid: a flat view of the seven continents of the real world laid out along lines of latitude and longitude, and a tightly coiled spiral line stretching and swirling on top of it. In other words, it's a spiral within a grid. The grid, we've figured out, represents the real and concrete space of Earth. The spiral represents time, and spirals inward from the moment we left home (where it's cut off by the map's edges) to a beginning point right in the center, which we can only suppose marks the beginning of history. The spiral circles inward above the map of continents, coiling too many times to count. (I suppose magic makes this possible; it seems there are an almost infinite number of coils. Germ says she doesn't really "get" the map, but I think it's kind of beautiful and symbolic.) And there is always a tiny blue glowing whale marking the location of Chompy somewhere along it.

Swimming the Sea of Always—for a time whale, at least—works like this: if you want to get to South Africa 1890, you follow the spiral around and around past that general location on the map over and over until you get to the coil of spiral that also represents the time you want to reach. Of course, to travel the entire spiral, or to pass every moment in history, would take too long to contemplate, but Chompy takes shortcuts—veering right across from one section of the spiral to another, though what his plan is when he's taking these twists and turns, we don't honestly know.

Floating words to the left of the map spell out where we are in time, to be helpful. Right now, apparently, we're swimming past Yugoslavia, 1990. In the upper right corner of the map, our destination is also spelled out in floating letters: San Francisco, 1855. Beneath that is our days until arrival: six. *Six* days, whale time . . . and Germ still sleeps like a log, while I go hot and cold every time I see that number get lower! Six days until my chance to steal back the precious person the Time Witch stole from me.

On the concave wall at the edge of this space, I have taped two photos: one of my mom and dad before I was born (and before my dad died), provided by Chompy. The other is one I brought aboard myself, an old-timey photo of my brother (the only one I have of him) standing in front of an old building, looking beyond the camera. I think he was looking at the witch who keeps him prisoner, because he looks petrified.

My mom told me a few months ago, when the memory came back to her, that I cried for a month straight after he was taken. She said most newborns cry but that I was inconsolable, and looking back, she believes it was the loss of my twin that broke my heart.

The photo is all I have to go on, because it's the one clue the Time Witch gave me the night she set me her gamble: thirty days to save him. Thirty days that begin once we are off this timeless whale, days that will be tracked by the small hourglass hanging around my neck.

I turn and make my way back downstairs, to our room and my soft bed. I take my Harry Potter *Lumos* flashlight out from under my covers and shine it onto my bedspread, making a tiny, luminous bluebird appear. She is a witch weapon of my own making, and she is our only chance.

I snuggle into my covers and watch Little One waddle around over my feet. I flick her across the room to tidy up my bookshelf. Ever since we boarded, I've been teaching her silly tricks, having her fetch me snacks, or pencils, or anything else I'm too lazy to get myself. Now she looks at me—small, and shivery, and uncertain. "You look like I feel," I say to her.

I turn the flashlight off and roll onto my side and try to drift off. I watch Germ's back as she sleeps.

Sometimes I'm able to forget we are ten thousand leagues under the sea. Other times, I can't forget the ocean and its dark deep water beyond these walls. I listen to Chompy's groans, soft calls, and whale song that echo all around us. Germ often says he's singing us to sleep, but I don't believe it.

I start to drift off.

And then, something changes. I'm shaken awake.

As I blink in the dim light, I realize it's Chompy that's shaking. This time violently.

Germ tumbles out of bed, hair sticking straight up.

The vessel around us is shuddering, changing course. Chompy tilts backward with a sudden jolt, and I slide off my bed too.

We are rising. Fast.

"DESTINATION APPROACHING," comes a loud, detached computer voice from the Grand View.

"What's happening?" Germ gasps.

"I don't know." I untangle from my covers and pull myself toward the front of the ship and up the steps. On the monitor, the ocean is still and empty. The destination still says San Francisco, 1855, six days.

"ARRIVING AT DESTINATION," the voice says.

"We gotta get ready!" I gasp.

I run, slide, stumble back to my bed as we feel Chompy level out. I snatch my flashlight, stuff it into my pocket, and wrap my fingers around my hourglass necklace nervously.

Chompy rocks to a violent stop, and my heart drops to my stomach.

It's about to begin. Our war against the witches. Too soon.

There is a sound like a creaky door as Chompy begins to open his enormous mouth.

"Act normal," I say quickly to Germ, though we've been over this before. "This is gonna be a busy, hot city, full of people from 1855. Some of them may have the sight. If we run into anyone who takes notice of us, never, *never* tell them who we are."

Germ nods, and then points to the hand I hold at my collarbone. My hourglass has leapt into motion. Sand has begun to trickle into the lower half. As it enters the bottom half, the sand transforms into a deep red liquid that floats within the glass, and slowly spells out the number thirty. I swallow. The blood-red thirty spins slowly, so that I can see it from all sides. It's like a tiny version of the holograms of the Grand View, only creepy instead of magical.

Normally fearless, Germ has gone ghostly pale with nerves as she sees it too. We are just at the surface of the sea, and water begins to trickle in at our feet. It is so frigid, it takes my breath.

And then I realize that maybe I'm supposed to give a pep talk. I am the last witch hunter, after all.

"We're ready for them," I say. "We know where we're going, and we know what we're looking for, and we know Little One can do this."

Germ nods, trying to look convinced.

I stand poised, with my weapon ready.

And I find I am, altogether, wrong.

We are not ready for this at all.

Chapter 2

We gape, standing frozen in the mouth of the whale. It is breath-shatteringly cold as we stare across a white expanse of tundra covered in snow—distant, jagged cliffs clawing at the dark sky beyond. Ghosts roam the windswept plain before us, moaning. Even the ocean waves around us move strangely: still and calm and flat one moment, then lapping wildly at Chompy's sides the next.

Ever since I burned my childhood stories in frustration (and accidentally got the sight in the process), I've been able to see a ladder dangling from the moon. (One night, I even climbed it to meet the Moon Goddess.) But now, up above, the moon looks like a cold distant marble, smaller and farther away than I've ever seen it . . . and there's no ladder, no sign of the Moon Goddess, at all.

Even the sparkling Beyond—its unknowable depths holding the spirits of those who've died and moved on—has gone hazy, like a gray fog has obscured its pink dazzle. If there are misty, watchful cloud shepherds guiding clouds through the sky, I can't see them.

Still, the marble moon gives off just enough light for us to see several silhouettes standing on the cliffs across the snowy expanse in front of us. The shapes begin to howl. *Wolves.*

Germ and I look at each other.

"Do you think this could be San Francisco?" I ask Germ.

Germ looks doubtful. She's about to respond when we both see it: a different kind of silhouette, moving on the cliffs amongst the wolves—a human one. The figure is holding a flickering lantern, orange and inviting in the dark, but a moment later the flicker disappears. We watch the dark shape hurry along the cliffs and disappear behind a jagged outcropping of rock. Whoever it is, they don't want to be seen.

"A witch?" Germ says.

I don't know, but it seems like if a witch saw us, she'd attack, not rush away.

"Whoever it was," I say, "this feels like some kind of trap."

"Chompy wouldn't do that to us," Germ says. I repress the urge to roll my eyes.

"We should get back inside," I say.

We step backward, deeper into the warmth inside the whale. And I realize I don't know how to command Chompy to close his mouth, to leave, to do anything really. The first time we climbed aboard, he did it on his own.

"Chompy, can you please get us out of here?" I ask.

But nothing. Chompy is perfectly silent, his mouth stretched wide and still. And all I can think is, *This is the whale who knows to provide copies of* Pet Psychic *magazine for Germ, but he won't carry us away from a deserted, frigid tundra we clearly don't belong in?*

"Let me try," Germ says. She closes her eyes and concentrates.

"What are you doing?" I whisper, still eyeing the shore.

Germ pops one eye open and looks at me. "ESP. I feel like Chompy and I have a bond."

But several moments of Germ doing ESP, not surprisingly, make exactly nothing happen. We stand there in limbo, unable to go backward, and knowing forward looks too un-survivable to contemplate.

And then Chompy lets out a giant breath, and we go flying out of his mouth, through the air. We land on the edge of the snowy shore. My *Lumos* flashlight tumbles a few feet away from me.

We sit up, panting, and gape back at Chompy in shock. Before we even know what's happened, he *chomps* his mouth closed and sinks beneath the surface of the water. I pull up my whistle on my wrist and blow it, soundlessly. Nothing happens.

The ocean grows as still as a lake. He's gone.

"I knew it," I gasp. "I knew we couldn't trust that whale."

We are alone, stranded on a barren and frozen island, in clothes meant for lounging about on La-Z-Boys. We won't last an hour in this cold. I am already so frozen, I can't feel my feet.

"What do we do?" Germ says.

"We find whoever was on those cliffs," I say finally, rolling toward my flashlight and snatching it up with fingers already going numb. "It's our only choice."

But, looking toward the cliffs, I don't know how to begin. Everywhere snow is lifted and drifting back and forth in the wind; if there were any tracks on the cliffs, they're probably gone. The few ghosts I could see from Chompy, whom we might ask for advice, have floated away—too far to reach.

And then I remember. My heart flutters with a tiny hope as it always does when I remember what Little One can do. I turn her on. Bright and luminous, she perches in the snow, looking up at me, unbothered by the cold and waiting for my command. It's comforting to see she's okay even while Germ and I are soon to be on the verge of hypothermia.

"Little One," I croak, "find whoever was on the cliffs and lead us to them. Fast."

Little One takes off like a bullet. She returns only seconds later, chirping for us to follow. Germ and I huddle against each other, taking a last look at the place in the water where Chompy disappeared (he might be halfway to the Bronze Age by now, for all I know), steeling ourselves to set off into the brutal frozen wilderness. Above me, I can see out of the corner of my eye, something shimmers, hums, and darts away. It's gone before I can catch a real glimpse of it. Little One chirps once and then goes quiet, waiting.

We wrap our arms around ourselves against the cold, and follow.

• • •

We stumble through the snow for what feels like hours but must only be minutes. I nearly cry with relief when up ahead a shape comes into view, the same shadowy human figure we saw before, hurrying along—perhaps unaware that we are following. The person is distant, but we can see that they are deeply concealed in thick warm clothes of some sort, and hooded. A few more minutes of walking, and we see what must be their destination up ahead: a small wooden hut nestled halfway up the cliffs at the water's edge, with one light burning bright in a window. The cliff is almost flush to the sea, in the shadow of an enormous white cruise ship marooned in the shallows, anchored and rusting and tilting precariously. I see ghosts drifting along the decks. Seeing it—how abandoned it is—gives me a sense of foreboding. It's another thing that feels wrong.

The figure climbs a treacherous set of stone steps that leads up the cliffs, and disappears into the hut. Little One lets out an excited volley of chirps. Beside me, Germ's teeth are clacking together so violently, I can feel the vibration as our arms touch. We look at each other. We might be walking into a trap, but the idea of getting out of the cold outweighs everything. We push on.

"Remember," I say, teeth chattering as we pick our way carefully up the steps, which are icier and more treacherous the higher we go, "whoever it is, they can't even see us unless they have the sight. That's what the time rules in our *Welcome to the Sea of Always* book said. But if they *can* see us, we tell them we're lost. Maybe . . . a shipwreck. Nothing about witches or hunting or anything else. Nothing about who we are. Right?"

Germ nods.

The wind begins to blow harder as we reach the hut. We try to peer through the windows, but they are so fogged from the warmth—*warmth!*—inside that we can't see through them. Finally, throwing caution to the wind, we pound on the door. No one answers. We look at each other again.

Slowly, with numb fingers, I grasp the door handle, and turn . . . slowly, slowly. My heart pounding, I push it open, and we step across the threshold and into the room, closing the door against the cold behind us. We gulp the warm air while we take in what we see.

We are in a simple room, rugged and rustic. A fire blazes in a fireplace in the corner. There is a simple single bed, a stack of wood, something that smells good cooking in a pot on a stove. There are musical instruments everywhere:

a guitar, a flute, a banjo. And standing on the other side of a small round table, there's someone watching us. The figure is still obscured by the leather parka, face wrapped in a scarf so that only the eyes are visible. Whoever it is can obviously see us . . . so either our time rules are wrong or this person has the sight. I can tell, because they're pointing a slingshot loaded with a jagged rock right at us.

A strong female voice emerges from the muffled scarf. "Tell me who you are, or you'll each lose an eye."

Germ shifts from foot to foot and looks at me.

"Um, I'm Rosie and this is Germ," I sputter. "We're travelers. . . . We need help. . . ." The figure in the parka doesn't budge, and the slingshot is still aimed squarely at my face. "Can you tell us where we are?"

But she doesn't answer us. She only narrows her eyes, which flash to Germ.

"I want to hear from this one," she says, nodding at her. "How did you get here?"

Germ looks at me. My heart in my throat, I wait for her to answer.

"Um, by ship?" she says.

"There hasn't been a ship in this port for over five years," the woman says.

I open my mouth to speak, but she shoots me a look.

She's the kind of person who, when she shoots you a look, you keep quiet.

"Um . . . ," Germ says. "Ummm . . . well, we came on a"—she looks at me—"really *small* ship. Like . . . a canoe. You probably didn't notice."

There is a long heavy silence. I can't be certain, but I think the figure rolls her eyes. Finally she speaks again.

"I know you came by whale. I saw you. Which means you've come from some other time. So you might as well tell me who you are and what you're doing here and how you got your hands on a time whale in the first place."

She says this all to Germ, who's clearly become her soft target. (If there's one thing this stranger is, it's a good judge of character.) At the words "time whale," Germ's eyes widened.

"We'd rather not say," I interject. I shake my head ever so slightly at Germ. "We'd rather know who *you* are."

The woman hesitates. And then she lowers her hood and slides off her leather parka, and reveals that she is not a woman at all but a teenage girl, maybe fifteen or sixteen. She's tall and willowy, black curly hair pulled back in a bun.

"Well, if you could have ended up anywhere," she says, this time definitely with an eye roll, "you've come to the wrong time." She points to the world outside, to the marble of the moon, the hazy fog-covered Beyond, the wild and wrong sea. "I'm Aria," she says. "Welcome to the witch-ruled world."

CHAPTER 3

Aria works over the stove, ladling whatever's in the pot out into bowls.

"My sister, Clara, always said we should feed anyone who came across our threshold, no matter how unwelcome. So there you are. Fish stew."

She practically throws the bowls onto the table. Germ and I peer into them, then at each other. We're not hungry, but the warmth of the soup is tempting. Aria moves back to the stove for her own bowl with a kind of confident tread, brushing escaped puffs of hair occasionally from her freckled brown cheeks.

"Um . . . thanks?" Germ says, not sure what kind of manners to use with someone who clearly wants us gone. Aria kind of reminds me of Germ's older brother David, who is generally annoyed by our existence.

"Where . . . when . . . are we?" I ask. "How do you know about time whales and witches? Do you have the sight?"

Aria ignores the last question, maybe because it's too obvious. "It's 2062." Germ and I gasp. Chompy has taken us many years ahead in the future.

"You're on the island called Mari, eighteen hundred miles from the nearest continent, in the middle of the emptiest part of the Pacific Ocean." She sips her stew as she watches us, openly suspicious.

"Does anyone *else* live here?" Germ asks.

Aria shakes her head. "Clara—my sister," she reminds us, "brought me here when I was seven. We were the only ones. I've been here ever since."

"But why *here*? Why so far from other people?" I ask.

Aria looks toward the window, her gaze growing heavy. "Clara said the world had gotten too dangerous. The weather has gone wild; wild animals roam the cities.

And the witches . . . With the moon getting farther and farther away, they've gotten fearless. Its light is too dim to deter them from cursing anyone they like, at any time. People are more and more careless about each other and nature. . . ." She presses her lips together slightly.

"Though, to be honest, I don't know what's happening beyond these shores anymore. And it's not like anyone can escape it, not really. This used to be a tropical island; it's *not* supposed to be frozen solid. The moon isn't supposed to be so far away. All I know is that the witches have covered the world in so many curses, it's propelled the moon away from us, and things are . . . frightening. And it feels as if there's worse to come."

We listen in stunned silence. *In only forty years, the witches do all this?*

Aria is watching us, a slightly new look in her eyes. "But mostly we came because they were targeting and cursing anyone with the sight," she says. "We needed to hide from them, like you." I watch her eyes slide to Germ, and realize it a moment too late.

"Oh, we're not hiding. We're *looking for them*," Germ says matter-of-factly. As these last words leave her lips, her hands pause with the spoon, and her eyes dart to mine. She puts her hand over her face. I open my mouth to interject, but Aria holds a hand up to quiet me. She has gone deathly still. It's as if the air itself has gone tense and tight.

"I want to hear from *her*," Aria says, nodding to Germ, narrowing her eyes intently. "*Why* are you looking for witches?" She asks the question urgently, as if everything depends on the answer.

"Well," Germ says, looking at me uncertainly. And then . . . well . . . months of being cooped up on a whale with no one to talk to but me, and Germ being a natural extrovert, break her open, like a dam bursting. "Rosie's the last witch hunter left on Earth, and I'm, like, her . . . assistant," she gushes. "We've come because the Time Witch stole Rosie's twin brother when he was born. She wanted to end Rosie's family. But she didn't realize he had a twin sister and when she found out, boy was she mad. She kept yelling, 'Tricked! Tricked!' It was awful. And she told us where he is—in the year 1855—and now we're on our way to rescue him. It's like this giant game for the Time Witch; she says we'll have to kill all eleven of the remaining witches to get to him. But our whale, *Chompy*, messed up and brought us here, even though he's a *good* whale, no matter what Rosie thinks. He just sort of *malfunctioned* or something. Maybe if you could help us figure out *how* to be on our way, we could be out of your hair." She looks over at me. I am gaping at her. "Sorry, Rosie," she says. "You know I can't keep a secret. And she seems nice. I think we can trust her."

Germ thinks we can trust *everybody*, I think, scowling. But it's hard to really focus on anything but the startled, tense way Aria is looking at us now. It feels like something sharp and dangerous has landed in the room between us.

She watches us for another split second, and then, abruptly, she walks to the window to look outside. When she turns back to us, she's unreadable but intent. She's got the concentrated look of someone mentally adding up a math problem.

"Your whale, he must have brought you here on purpose," she says.

"Why?" I ask.

"Because . . ." And then she freezes. She's listening to the air. "Listen."

I try, but all I hear is the wind coming in off the sea.

Then I hear it too. A low, distant buzzing, growing louder.

Aria's eyes widen. "The Time Witch knows you're here," she says flatly.

She grabs her slingshot off the table, and throws open the door.

"We'll have to make a run for it. To the caves."

"Caves?" I say sickly, panic seizing my bones.

"A hiding place. Let's go." Within seconds she has pulled on her parka and hood and slung a sack over her shoulder. She throws an oversize parka and a fur over-layer at us from a corner of the room. Each of us takes one, and she flings open the door. The wind whooshes in, chilling our only recently warmed blood, and we bundle ourselves. I am suddenly shaking with fear.

She leads us down the treacherous stairs quickly, taking each jagged step as if it's been memorized through a thousand uses. Germ, who's agile, stays close behind her with ease, while I stumble my way down. We follow, freezing again, fanning out onto the snow at the bottom of the stairs.

"It's at the other end of the beach, there," Aria says, pointing. I see nothing but snow and cliffs in the distance.

We start hurriedly across the snow, but only make it a few steps before Aria stops sharply and looks up at the sky. Something glimmering and opalescent is spreading out there, coming from above the cliffs and moving in our direction. The strangest sound reaches us, like a billion tiny rubber bands being plucked at once. And it's growing louder.

I yank my flashlight from my pocket and bring Little One back to life. She appears on the ground at my feet, ready, alert, agitated. She flits up to my shoulder, chirping a warning.

Aria looks at Little One, then us, and then at a strange bubbling on the ocean's surface where we arrived in the first place. A smooth hump rises out of the water. Shocked, I realize it's Chompy resurfacing.

Aria looks toward the other end of the beach, then at Chompy lying at the ocean's edge, now fully aloft on the water, mouth open. She's gauging which is closer, the cliffs or the whale.

"What can you do with her?" she asks, nodding to Little One.

"Make her . . . really big," I say. "Big enough to eat things." Aria's face falls. She's disappointed. I feel, suddenly, unsure of my weapon—though a moment ago I thought she was magnificent.

"Change of plans," she says. And levels her slingshot at the sky. She shoves me at my back, toward Chompy. "Go!"

We run, all three of us, in the direction of Chompy's waiting mouth. We're sprinting toward him, but it's clear we won't make it in time. Whatever is descending upon us is too fast, too numerous. Like a giant arrow made of a thousand parts, it's diving toward us.

And now I see what the swarm is made of: hummingbirds, multitudes of them. Aria is right. The Time Witch has found us.

We're nearly fifty yards from Chompy when they are suddenly just overhead. I turn Little One toward them and, stumbling in the snow, barely manage to keep my grip as she blasts into the air. She rises fearlessly, streaking into the sky, growing, growing. I watch as she tears one bird, then another and another from the air, ripping out their throats with her claws as she goes. She's the size of a tiger now, airborne, her claws huge. I imagine her bigger, stronger, deadlier. She is soon the size of a horse.

Beside me, Aria fumbles to load her slingshot with a rock. (There's no time to tell her that rocks are no match for a witch.) With Little One as cover, grabbing anything that gets in our path, we run again. But the hummingbirds come on faster. There are twenty or thirty catching up to us, then a hundred, then hundreds of them. And even as Little One grows in size—she's now as big as an elephant—taking more and more hummingbirds out with each bite, they surround her. Over my shoulder, as we run, I see her struggle.

And then, with a terrible screech, she tumbles out of the air. She plummets to the ground, and is engulfed. I stumble too, the flashlight dropping from my hands.

Even Germ falls, fighting off hummingbirds with her fists as she plunges to the ground. They pummel us from all directions. I grasp my flashlight again and try to shine Little One. She only flickers and flares, writhing as the hummingbirds engulf her. I watch helplessly as our *one* weapon against the onslaught vanishes. We're not going to make it. We're beaten already.

Just as I lose sight of the world and the swarm of hummingbirds surrounds me, I see Aria finally lodge her rock in tight to her sling as she's knocked to her knees. As she yanks at her sling, she lets out a sound: a piercing, howling melody she screams into the air, as beautiful and shattering a sound as anything I've ever heard. She shoots her rock upward, and a bright light bursts out behind it, like a bomb shredding the sky.

At first I don't understand that the two are connected, the scream and the flash of blinding, bright light.

Thousands of hummingbirds fall from the sky, blown apart at once. They fall like ashes, every single one of them destroyed. The air goes silent and still, and the sky around us goes suddenly peaceful, dark, empty. We look at each other in shock.

And then, behind us, I hear something else—a deafening and earthshaking *groan*.

I turn in time to see it, the cruise ship in the shallows, tumbling sideways toward the cliff where Aria's hut resides. It falls with a breathtaking, gnashing sound, ghosts screaming from inside as metal collides with jagged rock. Water splashes in all directions as the cliffside crumbles down to the sea, Aria's hut and all.

We watch, stunned.

"No," Aria whispers. "Not again." And then she yanks me to my feet as Germ slowly stands up behind us.

"How?" I sputter, gaping at Aria as she coolly watches the last remnants of her home fall to the ground. Then she looks at me.

"You're not the last witch hunter," she says as she pulls me forward.

And we run toward Chompy's waiting mouth.

CHAPTER 4

The second we are in, the giant wall of Chompy's mouth slams closed behind us. In a moment we are diving and everything is thrown forward.

Collapsed on the rug, panting, holding on to whatever we can grab to steady ourselves, we see that one tiny hummingbird has managed to make it in with us, and is lying injured on the floor. Jerking up, I rouse Little One with the flashlight still clutched in my hand, and she pecks the hummingbird frantically. A tiny spark of light bursts against the carpet as the creature disintegrates.

I fall back, exhausted. We lie there, gaping at each other, as Chompy steadies out. Then Aria leaps to her feet and scrabbles up the steps to the Grand View.

"To the Narrows," she says, and the map flickers to life before her, casting her in a dim blue light. Germ and I look at each other. Can you really just tell Chompy what you want, and he'll do it?

And then we are rocked and tumbled as the whale lurches violently again, tilts, . . . and dives. We listen as the depths of the ocean envelop us. Long moments of silence pass as we wait for something terrible to happen.

"Your whale is fast," Aria says. "We might lose them yet. They can see us from the air, you know, to about a hundred yards deep. But we'll do our best."

"The hummingbirds? I thought you destroyed them all."

"Impossible. There are millions of them. But with any luck, none of the birds that found us made it back to the others."

I stand and hurry up to her side, having finally caught my breath. "How do you know so much about time whales?" I ask. The only thing we've successfully commanded Chompy to do so far is swim to 1855, and even that was already pinpointed on the map when we boarded.

Aria looks at me, then stares around the room as if taking in an old haunt. "I rode one once, a long time ago, when Clara and I came to the island. And Clara knew everything, including how to 'hot-wire' a whale to come get us. She never told me how. But I know that when you're commanding a time whale, you've gotta speak clearly and confidently, like you really mean it."

She descends the stairs and crosses to the bedroom, pulls her leather sack off her shoulders, and plops it down. Following her, I notice that our room has grown to accommodate a third bed, which has appeared across the carpet from mine. Aria begins unpacking her meager things onto it. It's like she's had a go-bag fully loaded even though she's been stranded on an island for years. She lays out her parka, her slingshot, some dried jerky—all practical items except for a small glass snow globe. This she cups in her hands a moment before sliding it gently onto a nightstand that's appeared beside the bed.

"What a day. I'm gonna need some chocolate," she says. Some chocolate appears on her pillow, in a blue velvety box with a magenta ribbon. I notice that Aria's bed is somewhat nicer than ours. It's got a silk comforter and a million pillows. The lamp on her nightstand is vintage, as is the nightstand itself, and a set of speakers appeared beside the lamp in the moment I looked away. Posters of cool-looking bands I've never heard of have appeared on her wall. Suddenly music comes on—something indie.

Aria sinks down onto the bed with a sigh and immediately opens the chocolates, puts one into her mouth, and savors it, then runs her hands along the silk comforter. She re-twines her curly black hair into a bun at the back of her head, as elegant as a ballet dancer.

Germ and I watch in awe. And I think, *This is what a real witch hunter is like.* She takes each of these luxuries as if she expected them, with a bedrock kind of self-assurance. In five minutes she's made herself more at home on our whale than we have in eighty-eight days.

"How did you do that?" I ask.

"Do what?" Aria asks, chomping on chocolate.

"Kill the hummingbirds, save our lives, destroy that entire ship?"

Aria clenches her lips together for a moment at the last words. And I see a flicker of that self-assurance disappear. But then with a flick of her head, she shakes the moment off.

"The ship was a mistake," she says. "My weapon is . . . on the fritz. But I'm a witch hunter, like you. Your whale brought you to me on purpose, to save you. He must have known that wherever you landed in time, the Time Witch's hummingbirds would be watching. So he brought you to me. He's gotta be the same whale that delivered us to the island years ago."

"I think he's partial to me," Germ says. "That's why he wanted to save us."

Aria shrugs.

"I don't understand any of this," I say.

Aria looks up at me from under her eyebrows. "The Time Witch set you a game to go and rescue your brother in 1855?"

We nod.

"How long did she give you to complete your task?" she asks, casting her eyes at Germ for a moment.

I hesitate, trying to take it all in. "A month," I finally say. "Thirty days. Not counting our time on the whale, of course."

Aria looks at me solemnly, then looks at the space at the top of my collarbone, and nods, reluctant. "Look how much time you have now."

It takes me a moment to realize it's my hourglass necklace she's nodding to. I reach down to look at it and gasp. It looks like a third of the sand is gone now. In the globe of the bottom half, the spinning, blood-red, glowing number is now *twenty*.

"The hummingbirds stole time when they engulfed you," she explains. "They sucked ten days away from you. You've been witch touched already."

I think back to the night the Time Witch came to my room, long after I'd killed the Memory Thief and I thought the witches might have forgotten me. I remember how I opened my eyes and she was there, waiting with her photo of my brother, her dare for me to come find him. She must have laid a hand on me then to curse me. A witch can only curse someone by touching them, as if leaving a scent. But now touched, I am cursed forever, and her birds can steal from me with ease.

"What was your plan . . . once you got to 1855?" Aria presses.

"To have Little One devour the witches one by one," I say, holding up my flashlight.

Aria rolls her eyes. We have known her less than an hour, and already I feel like she's rolled her eyes at us at least twenty times. She's clearly unimpressed with me changing Little One's size.

"That doesn't happen."

"How do you know?"

Aria leans back. "Well, for one, you don't think the Time Witch would be ready for that? She's the *Time Witch*;

she knows everything before it even happens. She'd notice if someone tried to devour all the witches of the world one by one using a magical bluebird." She sighs. "No wonder your whale brought you to me. If I hadn't been there, your whole month would already be gone. Your chance at saving your *brother* would definitely be gone." She looks almost sorry for us, though still kind of annoyed in a teenager way. "You really don't know what you're doing. You were headed for certain death, for sure."

She yawns, and eats another chocolate. Germ and I stand there feeling ridiculous, and Germ gives me a look. It's obvious what we are both thinking. *She's so cool.*

"And now?" I ask.

"And now it's only *mostly* certain," Aria says. She tilts her head. "A witch once killed—anywhere in time—is killed forever; she couldn't go back in time to fix *that*. *But*, like I said, you kill one, and she'll be right there the moment you do, ready to pounce. On the other hand, if you go straight to 1855 San Francisco, all the witches will ambush you at once. I'm sorry, Rosie. It's over before you've even started. You're a mouse and she's a cat; she's just toying with you. It's kind of her thing.

"You're better off going back to the when you came from, going back to your time and living with your losses and finding a way to move on. Hope is a trick, Rosie."

Aria's words sit on me like a pile of stones. Of course the Time Witch would have known where we were headed and what we planned to do. How could I have been so foolish?

"For another thing," Aria says, plunging on, "I live in *your* future. And you saw what it was like."

I think about the future I've just seen, a world covered in ice, with a faraway moon and a Beyond gone dim. As Homer—our local ghost gossip back home—once told us, the witches are always using their curses to tilt the world toward darkness. They want to capture the world in a web of darkness and break the magical thread of connection that runs through all things, sending the moon and its goddess spinning off into space. Only, now I see it's happening faster than I ever dreamt.

"In *your* future," Aria goes on, "I know that only two witches have ever been killed."

"The Trapper . . . ," I say, because I know that my grandmother killed him.

Aria nods. "And the Memory Thief," she finishes for me.

"The Memory Thief's the one Rosie got," Germ says offhandedly, reaching out to touch Aria's silk comforter admiringly.

Aria goes still. It's the first time Germ has said anything that has caused Aria's eyes to go wide instead of roll. For the first time, it's Aria's turn to be surprised.

"Well, I'd like to hear *that* story. But for now, we've got some big choices coming up. And I need a nap before that happens."

"What kind of choices?"

But Aria doesn't answer. She pulls a silk eye mask out of her nightstand and arranges it on her head, perched at the top of her forehead.

"I don't skip naps," she says. Then she reaches to one side of the room, where a red velvet privacy curtain is hanging where it wasn't before. She pulls it as a divider between our space and hers. And all goes quiet.

Our new passenger rises just before dinner that evening, and appears at the table as Chompy fills it up with food. By then I have a million questions for her. Who and where is her family? If she's a witch hunter too, does that mean there are more? If so, does she know how many there are and how to reach them so they can help us? But Aria doesn't meet my eyes as she approaches the table; she's listening to music on a pair of headphones and is generally aloof to both of us. My questions catch in my throat.

Tonight, instead of the usual spaghetti or burgers or other things we love, the table fills with what looks to be *fine* cheeses, steaks, fresh baked bread, cherry turnovers, something Aria says is penne à la vodka, filet mignon, and so on.

"Ah, I've missed whale travel," Aria says. "Even as a kid, I had a taste for the finer things."

Germ and I don't know whether we should be insulted or excited that Chompy prefers to feed us junk food. But Aria, while she eats ravenously, keeps her eyes sliding upward to the Grand View, watching for signs of danger. She keeps one hand poised near her slingshot, ready to jump into action at any moment.

Even though I've always hated fine cheeses, I try to look like I know what I'm doing as I take a big slice of a green moldy-looking one and shovel it onto a cracker. Germ makes a grossed-out face at me, but I ignore her. *A real witch hunter probably does not live on Pop-Tarts,* I think.

I keep lifting my hourglass necklace nervously, making sure again and again that the grains of sand have stopped falling, now that we are back in our timeless vessel.

"So I've gotten us clear of the witch attack," Aria says, dabbing her mouth with a cloth napkin and sliding her headphones onto her lap, "but now, tonight, you're going to have to make a choice. We're almost at the Narrows. They're undersea cliffs with tunnels etched through the middle—enormous underwater gorges. It's the place I thought to take us because Clara told me it's one of the most hidden parts of the sea. The problem is, if we stay high above them, we'll be well within a hundred yards of the surface of the ocean, and there's a good chance the Time Witch's hummingbirds—if they're still in the area searching for us—will see us from the air. But if we go down into the Narrows where they can't see us, there are . . . other dangers. Giant sea creatures—some magical and deadly—volcanoes, the army of bones, dangers we can't even imagine . . ."

She trails off. Germ seems to have a sudden thought. She stands, crosses the room, and grabs the *Welcome to the Sea of Always* book. She flips through the maps and the rules of time travel to the two-page glossy spread that made us both shiver the first time we saw it:

The Pirate King and His Army of Bones. There is a fuzzy picture of a decayed pirate ship sunken underwater but still somehow sailing. It's taken from far off, as if whoever took it was too scared to get close.

"It says," Germ summarizes as she glances over the pages, "that the Narrows have been hunted for a *thousand years* by a pirate king who's put a bounty out on the head of any witch hunter. He's got a crew of hundreds of ghosts. He's pulled countless ships to their doom."

"Yeah, there's that," Aria says.

I feel my stomach flip sickly. Germ and I look at each other.

"Anyway," Aria pushes on. "You'll have to choose."

I swallow, hard. "Can *you* decide?" I ask. Aria is clearly far better at all this than I am, even if she did destroy half her island in the process of saving us. I basically want her to decide everything from now on. And then I add, desperation making me bold, "And then can you help us save my brother? Or at least tell us if there are other witch hunters who could help?"

Aria looks at me silently, and then shakes her head sadly.

"I wouldn't know about other witch hunters." She pauses, thinking. "I *guess* I can help you with the Narrows," she finally says. "I don't think I have much of a choice. But . . . I can't help you save your brother. You saw what happened with my weapon." She pauses, squinting a little as if the thought pains her. "I was thinking you could simply drop me off after we're in the clear, somewhere safe and tucked away but nice and warm for a change. Barbados in the 1960s or something." Germ and I exchange a crushed look.

I scramble for something to say to change her mind, my pulse thrumming. "Maybe you wouldn't *have to* fight," I say. "Maybe you could just . . . stay with us? Help us decide things, navigate things until we get to my brother? We could make it worth your while. We could pay you in um . . . unlimited filet mignon?" I think helplessly. We really have nothing to pay anyone with. "Please. You can't leave us."

"Nah, I'm good," Aria says breezily. "There's really no chance you'll succeed. Sorry."

Then her eyes go to the gift basket. She hesitates, like she is having a little debate with herself. "I mean, I did think for a moment . . . well, you might have something on this whale that I'd really like to have."

"What?" I ask, curious.

Aria stands and lifts the gift basket, then sits again.

"If you want the shower cap, you can have it," Germ says to Aria, "but I have to warn you it's been used."

Aria blinks at her, shakes her head in annoyance, and then pulls an envelope out of the very bottom of the basket. She opens the envelope and tugs out a white piece of paper with an image of a red ribbon printed across the top.

"I'd like to have *this,*" she says. It's the first time I've heard her sound nervous. She hands it to me to read. "Clara said there was always one in the welcome gift."

I take it from her, and Germ leans over my shoulder as we read it.

Welcome! This voucher entitles you to one forever stop, anywhere and any-when in the past. Next to this sentence is an asterisk, and at the bottom the statement is qualified: *The usual rules of time travel apply. You will not be seen except by those with the sight, you may not cross yourself in time unless you either are a ghost or wish to create a troublesome wormhole, you may not tamper with the course of human history, and so on.*

We look at her. "What's a forever stop?" Germ asks.

"You get to go to any day you want, and stay there forever."

I stare at the paper. Beside me, Germ widens her eyes at me. "It doesn't feel right, Rosie. What if we need it for something else?" She looks apologetically at Aria. After all, we didn't even know we had it until a minute ago.

"What would you do with it?" I ask, looking at Aria curiously.

Aria's eyes grow sad, but she blinks the look away. "That's up to me," she says with a toss of her head. Germ and I look at each other again. "But I guess if you were willing to let me have it, I could help with planning, logistics. But if there's any witch-fighting, it will have to be up to you and . . . your bird."

I hold the voucher out to her. "It's yours," I say. "If you help us get to 1855 in one piece."

Aria smiles, relieved. "Thanks." She softens a little. "In return, I'll help you as much as I can."

I nod, swallowing.

She studies us thoughtfully. "So, do we take our chances with an army of bones that wants to drag us to our doom, or the hummingbirds above?" We look at each other in silence. "I'm gonna need to think about this," she says. "I like to listen to my gut. And I usually like to do that by looking at fashion magazines."

We spend the next hour mostly quiet, each in our own nervous thoughts. A fireplace has appeared at one end of the room, and hot chocolate warms on the stove. Aria must really love chocolate.

A mug appears for me even though hot chocolate is not really my thing. Chompy must know how much I want to do things like Aria does them. Already, posters of bands

I only vaguely know have appeared on the wall beside my bed. And I find myself rolling my eyes when Germ puts on her shower cap for her bath that night and asks me if she looks like a mushroom. Germ notices the eye roll, and gives me an odd look, like she's a little embarrassed for me. Which is funny considering she spent all last year falling over herself with caring what people in sixth grade thought of her. I guess we've switched places, but I try not to think about it.

Aria lies on her stomach on her bed, listening to music on her headphones and tuning us out, flipping through French *Vogue*s. I sit on the rug with my back to her bed and pull out my *Witch Hunter's Guide to the Universe*, as if reading it for the thousandth time will give me some clue as to what to choose. I scan the faces and names of the witches who are still alive, the terrifying and skillful images of them my mom drew: Miss Rage, Babble, the Griever, Hypocriffa, Mable the Mad, the Greedy Man, Convenia, Dread, Egor, the Time Witch, Chaos.

Colorfully dressed male and female witches fill the pages, some grimacing or making funny faces, while others have such menacing eyes that they are hard to look at. I scan the chapters I know so well, written by my mother long ago: "The Invisible World and Its Beings," "The Oaks and Their Weapons," "Legends," "Secrets of the Earth and Moon," "What Is a Witch?"

I don't realize Aria is looking over my shoulder until she sits up behind me.

"This is impressive," she says, and it occurs to me I should cross out "The Oaks and Their Weapons" and expand it to include Aria and her sister. She points, as I'm flipping past it, to a note I've made about the sight, how it allows people to see the invisible fabric of magic in the world and how it makes them shine like a beacon to witches. "You should add that there are ways to dim yourself so you don't shine so much. Clara taught me how to do it." She bites her bottom lip thoughtfully, laying her hand on the book for a moment. "I can fill in some of the stuff that's missing, if you want."

"Was your mom a witch hunter too?" I ask. It's clear, from things she's said, that Aria's mom is not around anymore.

Aria tightens her lips together, almost imperceptibly. "My parents died. I don't remember them. But my mom taught Clara most of what she knew."

My eyes trail to the snow globe sitting on her nightstand.

"Do you mind if I look at that?" I ask, my curiosity outweighing my shyness.

She studies me for a moment, hesitating. Then she lifts the snow globe carefully, as if it's her most prized possession in the world, and hands it to me.

I gaze at the peaceful, beautiful little scene within. It's an olden-days kind of village, covered in snow, the soft fluffy kind you want to play in and sled in and walk in under the moonlight. I shake the globe and watch the flakes whirl and fall around the tiny houses. For a moment, something strange happens. A light goes on inside one of the cottages, and then goes out again. I stare at it for several seconds, disbelieving.

"You saw it, huh?" Aria says. She takes the globe from me, peering into it. For a moment she is soft and vulnerable, not annoyed or exasperated. "I see it too, sometimes." A sadness plays at the corners of her mouth. "Clara got the globe at some hippie magic shop in Idaho, shortly before we made our journey to the coast. She was twelve, I was seven." She glances at me and then back at the globe. "The shop owner had the sight, knew all about witches. He said some witch hunter had won the globe from the Time Witch in a card game, and had sold it to him when she was down on her luck." She shrugs. "I think he only *said* that to get my sister to pay more. Which she did. I've never even seen evidence that there *are* other witch hunters."

"Same," I say, swallowing, "not any outside my own family."

"This guy said there was a whole league of them . . . ," she says, and then her voice trails off. "The League of Witch Hunters."

I stare at the globe. The light stays off.

"Clara used to watch it," Aria says. "That light. She was always puzzling over it. She was *obsessed* with it, actually. Never went anywhere without her snow globe, was always staring into it when she thought I was sleeping. She said if anything ever happened to her, I should take care of it."

Goose bumps prickle across my arms.

"*Did* something happen to her?" I ask quietly, nervous.

There is a long, tense silence. "She's gone," Aria says finally, shrugging her shoulders as if she doesn't care. The freckles under her eyes squinch inward a little. "And she's the worst." Her expression goes cold for a moment, and she puts the globe back onto her nightstand. "How does your weapon work, by the way?" she asks, changing the subject.

I turn on my flashlight where it lies beside me, and shine Little One, making her retrieve a pen from my bed and drop it into Aria's hands. "She's powered by my imagination," I say. And then sheepishly, because it sounds so silly, I say, "I make up stories. I made a story about hope, and it made her big enough to eat the Memory Thief." I look around at my books. I used to think I needed to grow up and realize that made-up stories were not all that important, but now I suppose the future of my brother—and possibly even the world—depends on my ability to wield them.

Aria doesn't balk at this. Instead it's the first time I see her really smile. "That's cool," she says.

"How does *yours* work?" I ask, nodding to the slingshot she keeps constantly at her side.

"Music," she says. "I sing." And then her lips compress into a thin line again, her freckles wrinkling around her nose. "But my power's broken, ever since Clara . . ." She trails off. "It . . . goes overboard. As you saw. If I tried to kill a witch, I'd as likely destroy half the city we were fighting in. It's not safe."

I think of the ship tumbling down, destroying Aria's hut and the cliffs with it. And I understand why Aria doesn't want to fight. I wouldn't want to either, if my powers did stuff like destroy my own house.

"Well, it saved *us*," I say.

Aria proffers a smile, but a sad one. "And I hate to be the bearer of more bad news, but I've been listening to my gut for the last hour, and my gut tells me *you've* got to make the choice about the Narrows, Rosie. And it's gonna have to be stat. We're coming up on them now."

We climb the stairs again and gaze at the swirling three-dimensional shapes that circle the room, showing us the ocean surrounding us. There's a breathtaking sight ahead—two towering sets of cliffs, one on either side of a deep tunnel that looks like a scar running right down the middle. It isn't the kind of place you'd ever dream of going into. It's the kind of place where anyone is bound to get trapped.

I take a deep, ragged breath, and I think—suddenly—about the Moon Goddess. How before we left home, I climbed the ladder to the moon to meet her, even though now it seems as if I dreamt it. I wonder if she can see us beneath the sea. I wonder if she is rooting for us right now, if she even cares. What would *she* tell me to do?

The thing about the Moon Goddess is that the moonlight she reflects is filled with a magical kind of hope (that can also burn witches), but she doesn't really tell people the right answers. I wish she would make the sky fall onto the witches; I wish she would send me a sign.

I tug on my hourglass necklace. I feel claustrophobic as I stare at the entrance to the Narrows. But then I think of the Time Witch, her reptile eyes, her merciless grin. The terrors of the Narrows must be awful indeed, but I know that the Time Witch is the most terrifying thing I've ever seen.

"The Narrows, I guess," I finally say uncertainly.

And Aria nods.

"Dive. Take the low route," she says firmly to Chompy. And this time the whale moves slowly, ever so slightly changing direction down, down, down.

The sea around us dims, and grows even quieter. Inside, the lights glow softer. Chompy is trying to go undetected.

"We'll have to hope he can pick the right way forward, and hope to go unnoticed by the things these caves hold," Aria says.

The fear has gone from a distant one to a chill that makes me shiver. The high underwater cliffs rise up on either side as we approach, glowingly depicted in the dark space that surrounds us, and the silence of deep water settles in. The mouth of the Narrows looms closer and closer. And then—our vessel feeling dwarfed by the size of the emptiness—we enter, and descend in the dark.

CHAPTER 5

We watch the images of the Grand View reveal the beasts that drift around us: glowing giant jellyfish with long tentacles trailing behind them, and blind sharks hunting within the dark crevices of the jagged underwater cliffs of the Narrows. By Germ's count (via Sharpie), we've been traveling for three days in this dark crevice that goes on, and on, and on. The glowing map of the Grand View shows us making a meandering line to the southwest across the spiral of time. We are constantly tense, watching for telltale signs of the pirate king and his army of bones, or the sunken ships of victims they've left behind. Every once in a while, as we dive to avoid an overhang of rock or a particularly large squid, Chompy begins to quake a little.

"Chompy can't go any deeper than this," Aria says. "There are places in the ocean so deep that even a magical whale can't survive them. The weight of the water above becomes too heavy to bear."

I swallow. As if being surrounded by the dangers I already knew about weren't intimidating enough.

Still, after so long of it being only me and Germ, it's nice to have another person around (including one who basically wants nothing to do with us). It's nice to hear another person's breathing in our room at night, especially when it's the breath of a fellow witch hunter (even if she *is* a broken one).

Aria wakes us up each morning with a vigorous shake as if there's no time to waste, despite the fact that we're living in a timeless vacuum. She has the pragmatism of a girl who's lived alone in a frozen hut for seven years, and yet she can tell whether the pastry Chompy serves us is French or Italian. She keeps telling us that too many Doritos will give us worms, but we suspect she is messing with us.

She spends half the time sitting with a purple marker in her hand and combing through *The Witch Hunter's Guide to the Universe*—nodding at some things, shaking her head at others. She corrects anything we've got wrong or incomplete.

She has stapled in a blank page and created a section called "Time Whales and the Sea of Always," which has been conspicuously missing because, until a few months ago, I thought time travel through the sea was a rumor spread by ghosts, and I'd never heard of a time whale. She's formatted the page to be a lot like the ones my mom wrote:

WHAT IS THE SEA OF ALWAYS?

Time on Earth does not disappear as it passes, but rather, it sinks into the sea, becoming an invisible layer of history hidden within the ocean. Just as-above-there is surface reality and then the magical layer underneath, in the sea there is the real ocean and the invisible ocean of time. Still, the time ocean is very real in its own way, and any changes to time inside the sea will impact the course of history above.

WHAT ARE TIME WHALES?

Time whales are magical creatures adapted to swimming the magical sea. For most living things, swimming in the ocean won't mean swimming through time. But time whales have an inner space-time compass that has evolved in them alone, which allows them to navigate time's spiral.

Time whales are naturally hospitable creatures and are magically equipped to provide whatever their riders need. In witch hunters' cases this might mean a living room and favorite foods. In the case of witches, it might mean darkness and emptiness and the smell of despair in the air.

WHAT ARE WHALE WHISTLES?

To aid herself and her fellow witches in their tasks, the Time Witch used her skills to create whale whistles, a whistle for each witch to keep in her robes. She fashioned each one out of silver and space-time, carving a shell on the surface of each with her fingernail to mark it.

Any time whale called by a whistle must respond. And while most witches use the whales to spread curses through the past and hide from witch hunters, the Time Witch is fearless and instead prefers toying with those who would hunt her.

"The Memory Thief lost her whistle," I tell Aria as I watch her write. "My dad was a fisherman. He found it in his nets, and gave it to my mom."

Aria takes this in appreciatively.

Mostly I think we get on her nerves more than anyone else she's ever known. She picks up our clothes—which we tend to leave lying around the room, along with used napkins and dirty plates—as if she might catch something from them. She watches us stuff junk food into our mouths like she is watching a train wreck. When Germ insists that once a week we should have "sloppy joe days" because that's what they'd do at the school cafeteria back home, Aria just blinks at her and then turns and walks back into the bedroom and closes her curtain. At one point on the second day, Germ patted her arm and called her "Big Ar." It did not go over well. She's basically like the coolest big sister we never had.

Germ insists on continuing to make a mess, but I start picking up after myself. I start trying to do my hair in two puffed buns at the back of my head like Aria does (though, mine doesn't look as good because my hair is straight). And when Germ offers me Pop-Tarts one morning, I wrinkle my nose and opt for toasted brioche instead. I know what Germ is thinking: I've always harped on us being ourselves, and now I'm trying to be like Aria. But it's different, because Aria is a real, proper witch hunter, and I *need* to be one. I need to be calm, collected, and sophisticated instead of messy and daydream-y. In school, I was always Germ's sidekick, the unnoticed one. But now I'm supposed to be the leader, and I'm pretty sure getting it right means being a little bit less . . . *me.*

As tired as I am night after night, I don't sleep. I lie awake, shining Little One onto the ceiling above, making her larger, larger, until she is almost too big to fit in the room, before turning her off. I've seen how easily the hummingbirds defeated her, and it makes me anxious. Not to mention what Aria said: *You're a mouse and she's a cat; she's just toying with you. It's kind of her thing.*

We talk in circles about what to do, about how the Time Witch will know of any victory over a witch we have, the moment we have it, and travel back in time to stop me. Aria rightly shoots down every idea we have. I doubt right now that we could take on a pirate king and his army of bones, much less a witch. We are relying solely on luck.

Finished with the whale and whistle section, Aria turns the *Guide* pages back to the spread that shows the Time Witch—her pale white face, familiar reptilian eyes, her necklace of pocket watches. Germ has drawn a mustache on her, to make us feel better. Aria frowns. She adds a couple of lines here and there. In the end, the Time Witch's section reads:

> The Time Witch: Most powerful of the witches, besides Chaos. She is catlike, loves to play games and gamble with people.
>
> Curse: Manipulation of time. Like all other witches, the Time Witch must touch someone to curse them.
>
> Skills: Compresses, stretches, grows, and shrinks time. Makes people age too fast or takes away their ability to grow older.

Makes happy moments last less time and sad moments last more. She can hear time, and hear when the course of it has been changed by a time traveler. She sometimes steals scraps of time and tucks them up her sleeves.

Familiars: Hummingbirds, distinguishable by their empty blue eyes. They steal, distort, and warp the time surrounding their victims.

Victims: A person cursed by the Time Witch might age rapidly, or age in reverse. They might lose entire years without knowing it. Ghosts, fairly or unfairly, blame the Time Witch for their own angst-filled relationship with time.

I bite my lip, remembering how—the night the Time Witch came to my bedroom to set her challenge—her birds fluttered around me, and the time all around us went still: the clock, Germ's snoring, everything. It was like we were in a long and silent space between two beats of a moment. As soon as she left, time caught up again.

I don't relish thinking how simple it was for her and her hummingbirds to do that.

Aria turns to the last page, to the witch called Chaos. The drawing of him is not really a drawing of a witch at all . . . only a single black feather, like the feather of a crow.

"My sister called him the Nothing King," Aria says, pointing to the word "Chaos." "Has more of a ring to it, don't you think?"

I nod.

Aria takes this as a cue to erase "Chaos" and write "The Nothing King" in its place.

I nod, satisfied. If Aria called him "Mr. Pee Pee Pants," I'd probably still be on board, just because Aria said it. Anyway, Aria's parents passed things on to Clara that my mom, still recovering her memory, couldn't pass on to me.

> The Nothing King: The most powerful of all witches.
>
> Specialty: Nothing.
>
> Skills: Nothing.

Curse/familiars: Crows.

Victims: Everyone and everything.

It's kind of a funny entry, as if nobody really knows anything about him.

"Your guide is right that he's the worst of them," Aria says. "The Time Witch is nothing compared to the Nothing King. He's more powerful than all of the rest combined. But he's imprisoned in a black hole at the other end of the universe. He had a big fight with the Moon Goddess in ancient times, and she prevailed." She scratches her chin with the cap of her marker. "If he weren't locked away for all eternity, he'd be a real problem. Anyway." She shrugs. "With the Trapper and the Memory Thief gone, it's only ten more witches you have to get through, not eleven. He doesn't count."

Aria stares off into space for a moment, and a faraway look comes over her face. She's looking over my shoulder toward the Grand View, curious. We can see something blue and bright coming toward our ship.

"Huh."

She stands. We all move toward the Grand View to get a closer look, climbing the stairs.

A glow is emerging in the murky, foggy water up ahead.

The shape is hard to make out at first, the water is so dark, but as we get closer, its luminous glow reaches us so that we can see more fully what we are approaching.

"It looks like a cloud," Germ says.

"Not a cloud. It's too round. More like . . . the moon," I say.

My pulse begins to pound. The orb glowing ahead of us is beautiful. It does look, as impossible as it may seem, like the moon itself. My mind races for an explanation. Has the Moon Goddess sunk the moon to come and help us? The moment the thought crosses my mind, I am sure it's true, and my heart leaps inside my chest.

We do nothing as Chompy swims closer, as mesmerized by the light as we are.

All I can think is, *We're saved. We're saved. We're saved.*

We see the shape moving all around the moon, but not in time.

"What *is* that?" Germ breathes.

And then we lose our footing, because suddenly Chompy is jerking back. He lets out a rumbling, screeching sound underneath and all around us.

At the same moment, we see that the moon is not a moon at all but an enormous, glowing eye looking straight at us. Out of the shadows, swimming toward us so that now both glowing eyes are visible, is a squid as gigantic as any ship I've ever seen. There's a chain around its neck, tying it to one of the soaring cliff walls. And its tentacles, I see too late, are already stretching all around us!

"It's a trap," Aria breathes. "Chompy, rise!"

But it's useless. Chompy butts against something that slams down on top of him, and we fall with the stomach-dropping weight. He tries to slip backward, but that way too is blocked. And this time we see by what.

It's a rusted and glowing submarine with a hole in its side, and ghosts running to and fro along its decks and beyond its round windows. There's an enormous red skull painted at the nose. A net shoots out from the front of the ship, spreading like algae in the water.

"Swim past it!" Aria yells.

Chompy zigzags downward, and we narrowly miss the net as we dive for the depths below. But we see that this, too, is hopeless. We are diving straight into a pit, not a passageway. Inside it waits a pirate ship, completely submerged, sails torn. Hundreds of ghosts poke out of the windows and stand on the decks. They are going wild, like blood thirst has caught them in its grips.

The net settles around us now, and is dragging us down into the pit toward the ship. The light from the squid's eyes above disappears, and but for the glow of the countless ghosts surrounding us, the world around us goes black.

Already, ghosts are jumping off the ship and crawling all over our moonroof like ticks. We can hear the moaning of the dead as they begin floating in through Chompy's sides, appearing around the room.

I leap toward the bedroom to reach my *Lumos* flashlight, but two ghosts appear in front of me with rusted daggers. And as much as I've heard that ghosts can almost never hurt people, these two look very confident that they can.

"Wait for the king," one says.

My eyes dart to the flashlight on my bed. I am about to dive for it, right through them, when a figure appears behind them, and both spirits drift aside.

He is *dim*. So dim that he's nearly invisible. Frail. Withering. I can see at a glance, he is dying. Not the dying people do but something even worse. The pirate king is as *near to becoming nothing* as a ghost can get.

And Germ and I both suck in air at once.

"If you want to live," he says flatly, in a cold, steely voice, "you'll do as I say."

And then, so slightly that only I can see it, he gives me a wink. And I want to scream and wail and faint with joy at once.

The pirate king is Ebb.

CHAPTER 6

I'm so breathless, I might as well be a ghost myself. I would leap out to hug Ebb, but I'd fall right through him. Still, I jerk forward before stopping myself. Ebb's eyes are cold, as if he's never seen me in his life. My arms drop to my sides in confusion.

"How . . . ," I breathe. "How . . ." It's all I can get out. Beside me, Aria has her slingshot raised and is ready to smash a song-driven stone into Ebb's face (and also possibly sink our whale in the process).

"Ebb!" Germ says. "You're alive! I mean, not dead. I

mean, you're *dead* but you're not *nothing*! I mean . . ." Germ is wringing her hands, and her face is practically exploding with emotion. Ebb ignores her, and looks at the two ghosts beside him.

"I've heard the loud, light-haired one suffers from delirium," he says.

One of them points a hand toward Germ's hair. "We can remove the hair if it's a problem. Or the head."

Ebb shrugs. "The Time Witch will want them as they are," he replies. The other two nod, hanging on his every word. "Hurry to the ship," he continues. "Take the others. Steer to the surface, find her birds. Tell her we've got them."

"Ebb," I gasp. He shoots me a look, his eyes drilling into mine. I shut my mouth.

The pirates—all at once—drift out through the walls of Chompy and disappear. As soon as they're gone, Ebb's shoulders fall, and he looks at us.

"We gotta move fast," he says. "If we can make it through the gap, we've got a chance."

I don't have time to answer before he peers around and then steps up quickly to the Grand View, searching with darting eyes the holographic image of our surroundings that spin around him. We are not in a pit at all, it appears, but a set of caves that was not even on our maps a moment ago. And then, in the glowing blue shapes of the sea around us, we see a thin, crooked slit on a distant stone wall, with the vaguest hint of a silver glow within it. He points at it. "There it is. It's a tricky bit—a slit through time to another part of the sea altogether, a kink in the spiral. We only have a few minutes to get through it before they return." He looks at me. "Can you steer your whale there?" he asks. "Into that narrow gap?"

I look at Aria, who doesn't answer. Now that I've seen how *she* does it, I'm hoping I can do it too.

"I think so," I say.

Aria shakes her head. She's still aiming her slingshot at Ebb's face.

Ebb swallows. "You're going to have to trust me," he says.

"Trust a pirate who's sworn to have the head of any witch hunter on Earth?" she says. "I'd rather be dead."

His eyes flash at her. "You'll be worse than dead if you don't do what I say. Rosie, tell your whale to dive."

I hesitate. I don't know what's happened to Ebb, why he is so dim and empty-looking, why his voice is so steely and mean. And then I see Fred, his pet spider, crawling up the sleeve of his worn, ripped coat. It feels like seeing an old, close friend.

I look an apology at Aria, who is shaking her head at me.

"Through there, Chompy," I say, the way I've seen Aria do—with confidence, though my voice quakes more than I'd like. Still, just like that, the whale listens. Germ looks at me, and I raise my brows at her, as surprised as she is.

The moments pass as we swim toward the gap. We are diving into an emptiness. Either we are about to disappear into a fathomless nothing of a pit, or we're about to be delivered from danger.

And then, in another moment, we are in and through. Light suddenly cascades down through the water in beams. The darkness falls away behind us. And something unexpected opens out in the view beneath us.

A sunken, ancient stone city.

Ebb turns to us, and his anger collapses into an expression of physical pain. He winces, and as he does, he brightens and then dims—light, dark, light, dark.

"We'll be safe here. Also," he says, looking up at my double buns that I've made to be like Aria's, "what's up with your hair?"

And then he flickers out, and disappears.

He reappears a moment later, dim and drawn-looking.

"Rosie," he breathes. "Germ." He grimaces a smile. He looks at me, taking me in.

We are swimming over the rooftops of the underwater city. Germ says she thinks Chompy likes the view because he's making gentle whale sounds, like someone oohing and aahing at a museum. Sharks weave in and out of streets below us; algae covers what looks to be a temple. It's beautiful.

And then I notice, Aria is still armed and ready to thwap Ebb in the face. "Can someone explain to me how you all know each other?" she demands. "And why I shouldn't get rid of this guy?"

Germ must see this as her moment to convince Aria we're not the silly little kids she thinks we are. She suddenly hearkens back to an etiquette class we had in fifth grade.

"Aria, this is *Ebb*. Ebb, this is *Aria*. *Ebb*, Aria is the second-to-last witch hunter on Earth and enjoys fine chocolates and filet mignon. *Aria*, Ebb is a ghost who has haunted Rosie's house all her life, until the Time Witch got him. Also, he showed Rosie that the invisible fabric of the universe exists. He likes . . . um, *us* . . . and spiders . . . and listening to nature and trying to understand what it's saying." She turns to Ebb and blinks as she runs out of polite introductory things to say. "What are you doing here?" she asks. "Why are you pretending to be the pirate king?"

Ebb's eyes shoot to mine, then flick away.

"I *am* the pirate king," he says.

"But . . . ," Germ begins. There are so many buts. *But the pirate king has haunted the seas for a thousand years, and we only saw Ebb last June. But the pirate king does terrible things to people on behalf of the Time Witch. But the pirate king is evil.*

Germ gives me a look that says, *Awkward.*

"And what is this place?" Aria asks, cutting to the chase. "How do you know we're safe here?"

Ebb's forehead wrinkles in brooding thought, a familiar expression that I've missed for so long.

"I've uncovered so many hiding spots over the years, but this is one of the best. You stumble on these kinds of things, eventually, when you roam the sea for so long. This is the city of Helike, lost to the world above." He looks sad, and won't meet our eyes, as if there's a lot he doesn't want to say. "I don't think anyone knows about it really, even the Time Witch. It's absolutely forgotten by history."

Watching the city drift beneath us, I can easily imagine that no one remembers it. Sharks swim through the streets, and giant clams lie at the foot of elegant staircases. It looks like something out of a fairy tale.

Pulling my gaze from the view, I see that Chompy has already changed things to accommodate Ebb. There's a dusty attic-like space for a bedroom at the other side of the main room, some vintage things like an old catcher's glove and a pogo stick, and a prefab web up in the corner all ready for Fred the spider to move into. Ebb lifts Fred from his sleeve and places him on the web.

I watch him, mystified. How could a boy who's so kind to spiders menace the Sea of Always for a thousand years? But then I keep thinking how the other ghosts treated him: like a leader, and someone they were scared of.

"Fred's gotten dim too. It's all the years away from our grave," Ebb says, swallowing. "We're fading away. I thought it would happen a lot faster, to be honest. I haven't had a time-traveling whale like you, but life under the sea, it slows things down."

His words slice right through me. *Of course. That's* why Ebb is so dim. All these years, he's been away from his grave. He is fading into nothing at all.

"What happened to you after we last saw you, Ebb?" I ask. I feel sick, waiting to hear the answer. I may not want to know what it is.

Ebb flickers out for a split second, then reappears.

There's a long silence as he looks anywhere but at my eyes.

And then, of all the things I never expected to hear, Ebb tells us how he came to rule and terrorize the ocean of time.

CHAPTER 7

"Everything was so peaceful the night she took me," Ebb says. "It was dark moon, so of course I knew it was a riskier night with the moonlight gone, but it'd been so long since you'd destroyed the Memory Thief that I wasn't worrying about it. The witches hadn't come for you: no revenge, no attacks, nothing. I was starting to feel like you and your mom were safe.

"I remember you were up in your window that night, reading a book while your mom was cooking dinner. It was the picture of what I'd always wanted for you—a happy home, your mother's love. I was out on the grass by the cliffs, guarding the yard and your house, as usual. I guess I had gotten too comfortable with things."

He thinks and swallows. I can see fear pass through his dim frame and over his face, a kind of terror.

"One minute I was alone, and the next minute I just . . . wasn't. She was . . ." He pauses, then continues, "Standing there, a few feet away.

"It was her eyes I saw first, those empty blue eyes, gleaming in the dark across the lawn. I tried to move, but I wasn't fast enough. It was like she moved at the speed of light. You wouldn't believe how fast. And then her arms were wrapping around me. There was only time to think, *I'm gone.*" He shakes his head. "The only other thing I thought about was *you.* I thought, *She's after Rosie next.*"

He looks down at the floor.

"Anyway, the next thing I know, I'm in a cellar. I didn't know where or *when* I was, but there were other ghosts jailed with me: a ghost of a baker from Portugal in the 1600s, a ghost named Lin Mei who was a dancer, a professional thief from the 1970s named Steve. They told me everything: what year we were in—1018; and what place—some abandoned castle in what is now Spain. Basically, the

Time Witch keeps a few ghosts around to gamble with. I was one of those ghosts."

"Gamble with?" I ask.

"Sort of like poker chips. If she's gambling with someone, she'll bet them five ghosts, that kind of thing."

"But why would someone want ghosts?" Germ presses.

Ebb has made it clear many times that ghosts, unable to touch and move things except for in rare circumstances, are generally useless.

"Turns out some people with the sight like having ghosts around," he answers. "To sing to them, or be gentle alarm clocks, or be night-lights, or to keep the people company. And the Time Witch sometimes *gives* things to ghosts, half-magic, half-real things they can use to make them less useless. Like brooms for cleaning, stuff like that. She gave my crew their daggers."

"But why don't the ghosts just escape from her jail?" I ask.

"Lead walls," he says, his eyebrows lowering. "ANYWAY," he goes on, "I passed year after year in that cellar, waiting to be gambled away, hopeless. And you know me. I like to *listen*. I noticed the water whispering that there were tunnels under the lead cellar. The mold grew in a certain direction like it was trying to point the way out. It was like all the life in that cellar wanted to help me escape. Only, I didn't have the will.

"She caught me one day, when she came to collect another ghost she'd lost in a game of cribbage. She caught me whispering to Fred and listening. And I suppose it made her think she could use my services. She wanted me to try to teach spiders in the castle to be her spies.

"Well, she started having me come to different rooms upstairs to talk to the spiders and so on. And that's when I got more of the lay of the land—the layout of the castle, the fields all around and the ocean beyond. I spent a lot of time up there, and after a while she barely noticed me. By that time I think she'd long forgotten where she'd collected me, or why. I'm a ghost, *harmless and powerless*, you know?

"And every night, it was back to the cellar. The ghosts came and went, and passed the time with gossip, like they always do. I listened to that, too." He glances at his feet. "That's how, one night, I learned you were still alive. They were talking about a witch hunter, about the game the Time Witch had set for her." He looks up and meets my eyes. "They said the Time Witch had dared the witch hunter to rescue her twin brother. I knew it had to be you." He kneads his hands together. "They said you were doomed."

A long silence.

"Around that time, I started to develop my plan. Every night, the Time Witch would head out to spread her curses while I organized things at the castle—getting the insects to spy, getting the other ghosts to behave, getting more and more of her trust. When I told her I could whisper the creatures of the sea into attacking ships and whales, she was intrigued." He stares at his fingernails and looks up at Germ. "Basically, I told her I could organize the Sea of Always the way I'd organized her castle, have it all at her command. You'd be surprised how much of the sea—how much *nature*—is really beyond her control, so she was tempted by the offer.

"She gave me a ship. Really, what she wanted more than anything else was more weapons against any witch hunters who might come after her." He glances at me again. "Even the ones she invited herself.

"I gathered a menagerie of loyal sea creatures, and a crew of thousands of ghosts . . . the bad ones. You know, ghosts who'd done horrible things in life and never moved on."

I nod. I know all too well how some ghosts move on to what is Beyond, and some don't.

"I built my undersea army. Ghosts can't usually fight, as you know, but we had our witch-given daggers. *And* we had our nets, which the Time Witch also provided—

half-real and half-magic, like I said. And then . . ."

"And then . . . ?" Germ asks. We are both on the edge of our seats, wanting him to tell us that it's all a big misunderstanding, that he didn't do those unspeakable things we read about in our *Welcome to the Sea of Always* book. Then again, for Ebb a *thousand* years have passed. Enough lifetimes to change someone into a person—or a ghost—you don't even know anymore.

"Then what?" Germ finally demands. "Ebb, did you do all those horrible things the book says you did? Maraud the sea for riches, pull countless ships to their doom? Did you do all that to survive the Time Witch?"

Ebb looks at her a moment, his eyebrows low, and pauses for what seems like forever.

"If there's one thing I've learned over a thousand years," he says, "it's that ghosts like to gossip." And then he turns his eyes on me. "But you can't believe all the ghost gossip you hear." For a moment, his eyes have a twinkle. "I've encouraged my crew to, um, embellish our adventures a bit."

I see Germ visibly breathe a sigh of relief. I am pretty sure I do the same.

"Well, what about the squid?" Germ demands. "You've got him chained in the Narrows!"

Ebb shrugs. "You mean Inky? Oh, Inky's all right. He's

better at unlocking that collar than any ghost could ever be. He's very dramatic, a top-rated performer. I'm glad I took a chance on him."

He smiles at Germ and Aria, but doesn't look at me again. I get the feeling more and more that he's avoiding my eyes . . . that he'd avoid me altogether if he could. And I don't understand why.

"I've kept plenty of secrets from my crew. One of them is Helike, and another one is that I'm not out to kill witch hunters after all. They'll be enraged when they find I'm not on their side."

Aria, still looking distrustful, says, "I'm not so sure *ours* is the side you want to be on."

Ebb blinks at her. "What do you mean?"

Aria looks steadily at him. "Rosie's hopes of saving her brother are pretty much crushed. The Time Witch knows Rosie's every move the moment she makes it. It's a trap in every direction. Basically, your friends are beaten before they've started."

For a moment, an expression crosses Ebb's face that shows the old Ebb—moody, protective, determined—making an appearance at last. He pushes his flickering brown hair out of his flickering ghostly brown eyes.

"I can fix that," he says simply.

CHAPTER 8

We stare at Ebb. A tangle of nerves zings in the pit of my stomach.

"What do you mean, you can fix it?" Aria asks suspiciously.

Ebb puts his hands into his pockets. "I mean, all those years I was watching and listening to the moss on the walls, and the water under the floor, I watched and listened to the *Time Witch*, too. And I learned." He looks back and forth between Aria and Germ, and only occasionally at me. "I learned that witches wash their faces with dirt. I learned that some of them snore. I learned that even though they roam the Sea of Always in their whales, they hate water. I learned that the Time Witch likes to hide stolen scraps of space and time in random places; I know a ghost who says he found a forest from the 1700s that she hid in a sock once. And I learned something else, too."

By now he's looking a tiny bit full of himself. "This one night when I was up in her room, she opened this rusty square metal box she had beside her bed, like a jewelry box but really plain, and took something out of it. It was as if she wanted to look at it for only a second, to check on it. Then she stuffed it back into the box. It was the only time I ever saw her do that in two hundred years. But I'll never forget it."

"What was it?" Germ asks.

He smiles, and looks rather pleased with himself. "Her heart."

We all blink at him, speechless. "Her *heart*?" I breathe.

"Clara," Aria offers slowly, her eyes on Ebb, "once told me she'd heard that witches and their hearts aren't attached. That witches carry their hearts around, like accessories."

Ebb nods. "It's true. I'd heard the rumors, but I'd never given them much thought until that night. A witch's heart doesn't pump her blood, but she still needs it to live." He looks up at me. "In other words, if you destroyed a witch's heart, she'd die."

Aria gets up to go check the Grand View and then returns, as wary as always even in this hidden place.

"But this doesn't fix anything," I say to Ebb. "Even if we managed to steal a heart and destroy it, the Time Witch would know the second we did it, and she'd go back in time and destroy *us*."

"Well," Ebb says, "I was thinking that, but then I was thinking about fire ants."

"Fire ants?" Germ and I echo simultaneously.

"Well, there's this kind of ant that attacks its victims in a sneaky way. Basically, a whole bunch of ants crawl up a creature's legs, unnoticed, until they're all over its body. Then one of the ants sends the signal, and they all bite at once. It's like, they spend all their effort setting up the attack. Once they actually bite, it's too late, the animal is overwhelmed."

Germ looks conflicted. "Smart little guys," she says. "Also, poor animal. I don't know who to root for." Aria gives her a look like, *You can't be serious.* But Germ is the kind of person who can't help but root for both sides in any battle. (One time, she cried when I told her the basic plot of *Snoopy, Come Home.*) For now, she's been rubbing one of the walls as Ebb has been talking, so she doesn't notice Aria's look. "I'm giving Chompy a cheek massage," she says.

Finally we turn back to Ebb. "Okay, so what do fire ants have to do with killing witches?" Aria asks.

Ebb clears his throat, his full-of-himself expression melting under Aria's skeptical gaze. "Right. So yes . . . the Time Witch is one step ahead of you and always will be because she knows anything that happens at any time. So killing the witches one by one won't work, and neither would killing them all at once—even if you got the chance. You'd be no match for all those witches at the same time.

"But, well, I've had about a thousand years to think about this. And I was thinking, if the Time Witch is so careless with her heart, the others probably are too. I mean, witches are pure evil. They're not exactly *in touch* with their hearts, you know? I bet they all keep them somewhere nearby but neglected."

We don't answer because we don't know how. Ebb has taken on a brightness that was not there a few seconds before. For a moment he's almost as luminous as his old self, more *here* than gone.

"If we were to *sneak* somehow like fire ants do, to steal their hearts one by one—hearts they never check on anyway—the Time Witch would never know. Nobody would notice that their hearts were gone, not for a while."

And then he dims slightly. "I wouldn't be able to help"—he nods upward—"out there. I'd have to stay on board. Another day out of the sea with time passing, and I'd probably fade away completely. It would be up to you three."

There is a long silence as we take this in. Germ is the first to break it.

"And then what would we do with the hearts, once we have them?" she asks.

He shrugs, as if this is the simplest part. "We have Little One eat them. All at once."

"But then there's still the Time Witch," I press.

Here he falters, flickering a little with doubt. "We'd have to count on the element of surprise with her. I can't think of any other way. We go to 1855 as our final stop. She'll have all the witches there waiting to attack. What they won't know is that we're already holding their lives in our hands. We have Little One devour the hearts the minute we face them, and take advantage of the Time Witch's surprise to have Little One attack her before she can react."

We are silent.

It's actually kind of a good plan.

"How would we find them? All the witches?" I ask.

Ebb opens his mouth to reply. "I don't kn—"

"Whale song," Germ interjects. "Chompy can ask around." I look to Aria, trying to gauge whether this is a crazy idea or not, and surprisingly, she looks intrigued as Germ starts to think out loud. "The whales are probably friends, you know? *I'd* be friends with the others if I were a time whale. Just because the witches command them doesn't mean they don't like to chat with each other."

"They could tell Chompy *where* in time they last dropped off their witches," Aria offers. She's tense, but I can see her grudging appreciation of Ebb's and Germ's ideas. She's softening toward Ebb, for sure. "We'd have to make our landings on or around dark moon nights, when they're getting bold enough to be out and about. Obviously, the Time Witch would be keeping your brother in San Francisco on a dark moon night, so that one's a given. Then it's just a matter of stealing hearts from the nine most fearsome souls on earth before we get to her."

"Even if she's caught off guard, the Time Witch could have us cursed in a second flat," I offer. "She's the Time Witch."

Everyone nods grimly.

"I still think it's the best option we've got," Ebb says. His eyes dart again to my hair, in the buns. I'm beginning to feel self-conscious about them, and about him noticing how much I'm trying to be like Aria. I casually roll them out.

"There's one major drawback to the plan," Aria says. "If even one of the witches catches us stealing, notices what we're up to, it's over. We have to pull off all nine thefts perfectly, from nine terrible beings. And *then*, like you said, we still need to defeat the Time Witch. All before Rosie's remaining time runs out."

"The witches won't wander far from shore and the safety of being able to call the whales they command," Ebb offers. "They're lazy and scared of the moonlight and don't like to be out in the open for long. We could find them."

We sit in silence for a long while, all weighing the choice we face. Aria is the first one to speak. And her voice is softer, kinder as she looks at Ebb.

"Well," she says, "up till now this mission has felt completely impossible. Now it only feels *mostly* impossible." She tilts her head, smiling slightly, the kind of smile that might belong to a girl who has not given up on battling witches as much as she says. "I guess I could help, with a plan like that. Even though I can't help to fight."

Germ, too, is clearly warming up to the plan. Then again, Germ is always the brave one.

They all look at me, like I'm the person everything hinges on. I do not like being the person everything hinges on. I like to be the one watching from the wall.

"Ebb, the first place we're going is home," I say. Ebb is fading, and he needs to get back to the place where he died, to recharge.

"You can't," Germ says sadly. "The time rules."

She retrieves our *Welcome to the Sea of Always* book, opening to the rules page.

We scan the list, past the rule about tampering with the course of human history (I suppose witches don't listen to that one, and maybe since they're half-magical, it doesn't count) and the one that forbids any living person to cross themselves in time. Then Germ points to the rule she's remembering:

> *No extra stops beyond one's central mission, EXCEPT when using a forever voucher.*

"See?" she says. "The only way to make an extra stop is by using the voucher. And you promised the voucher to . . ." Germ looks at Aria, who shakes her head.

"I can't give it up. I'm sorry, I really can't."

Ebb seems to catch on vaguely to what we're talking about. He looks at the hourglass around my neck. "I've waited a thousand years. I can wait twenty more days, more or less."

But I can't help thinking about something that makes my stomach churn. If I hadn't promised Aria the voucher, we could have taken Ebb back to the time before he died. Not only could he have recharged, but he could have seen his parents again, before they died too. He could have spent a day forever with them.

Again, everyone is silent. They are waiting for me to make a choice.

I stand, and walk up to the Grand View to look at the old-timey photo of my brother, his wide eyes like mine, his fear at whatever or whoever lies beyond the camera.

The sea is peaceful and safe around us, and time on the whale stands still. We could swim the ocean for a long time trying to look for other solutions, safer ones, hoping to escape the Time Witch's notice. I am not like Germ and Aria. I could burrow into a hole with my stories and the people I love, and never mind not venturing out or saving the world at all, if only I could know that Wolf was okay. Then I would happily let someone else fight the witches.

"I need to think," I say. "It's gambling it all in one shot. It's risky."

"I get it," Ebb says. "But I'd say decide soon. My crew will be looking for us. The Time Witch will be looking for us. And there's something else." Ebb flickers. "Something more I learned about the Time Witch, watching her over the years. She's planning something. I don't know what, but whatever it is, it's more than just covering the world in darkness. There's something deeper she's trying to do."

"Deeper than covering the world in darkness?" Aria looks dubious.

"I know it sounds weird. It's nothing I can put my finger on exactly. Only . . . something's up. Something we don't understand."

We all take this in uncertainly, because it's hard to get upset about something possibly worse than fighting to save the world from a web of evil that, in Aria's time, has sent the moon spinning away.

"Well, if we kill them all," Germ says, looking on the bright side, "we'll never have to find out."

CHAPTER 9

Several days pass as we go over and over the possibilities, safe and static on our whale as he circles the hidden backwaters of the city of Helike.

Aria and Ebb carefully lay out what our plan would look like if we *were* to go through with it: the amount of time we'd have to steal the heart of each witch (about fifty-three hours per witch, on average, which doesn't seem like much when we don't know how far inland we might find them), and how we'd go about doing it unnoticed by witch spies.

Aria explains what she learned from her sister about

the sight. To dim the sight so that witch spies and witches don't see you, you basically close your eyes and imagine turning down the volume of your *inner self*, as if you were using the volume on a remote control.

"To be clear," she says one evening, "dimming yourself *won't* make you *invisible*, especially not to a witch. It'll just make it so you don't shine out to her and her familiars like Rudolph the Red-Nosed Reindeer. We will need to be sneaky."

As I listen, I fiddle around with Little One, whipping her around and making her dart faster, grow bigger, dive, bite, grab things around the room. I know she's going to have to be the key to all our thefts, but I'm not exactly sure how. With the Memory Thief, I made Little One enormous. But there's nothing sneaky about a luminous bird the size of a house. Not to mention that after what happened with the hummingbirds, I'm afraid she's not as strong as I hoped.

Ebb and Germ and Aria go on talking, but quietly enough that I can't hear. They giggle about something together. In the three days since he boarded our whale, Ebb has ignored me almost completely—leaving conversations when I join them, not looking me in the eye. There are things I forgot about him, like how he blushes brightly like a lamp when he's embarrassed, and how curious he is about everything. Now, feeling hurt, I watch the three of them chatting so easily. Whatever makes him avoid me, it's not impacting his friendship with Germ or his getting to know Aria.

I know I should ask him. But I'm pretty sure I can guess the reason why he doesn't seem to like me anymore: I'm the girl who let him get caught by the Time Witch. I'm the one he was trying to protect, and instead it got him a thousand years wandering the world alone, and nearly got him obliterated.

Eventually Germ comes and perches on my bed, crossing her arms around her knees and looking at me.

"How's it going with Little One?" she asks.

"I'm trying to figure out how we'd use her to get the hearts in a sneaky way. But it's hard because . . . I don't know what to expect, you know?"

Germ nods. She looks me over. I'm wearing pj's that are almost an exact imitation of Aria's white silky ones.

"You don't have to be like Aria to be a good witch hunter, you know," Germ ventures, like she's walking on eggshells. "I mean, Aria's great, but so are you."

Dubious, I glance over at Aria as she chats with Ebb. Not only does she know everything about witch hunting, but she's also better than I am at being friends with the ghost who's looked out for me my whole life.

"I wish I was as good at making friends as you guys are," I say. Even back home, I've been trying to be more outgoing with Germ's huge and growing array of friends. But it's not as easy for me as it is for her.

Germ is thoughtful. "I'm no witch hunter like you and Aria, so what do I know . . . but maybe you don't need to be friends with *a lot* of people, just the right people." She pauses. "As for Ebb," she says, looking over at him, "whatever his problem is, he'll come around."

I want to think Germ's right. But I also wonder if I will never be quite the right fit anywhere. And I wonder how someone who's not the right fit anywhere can save the world.

Germ is sitting and watching as I make Little One swipe a dust mote out of the air, when we both look up to find Ebb watching me.

"What are you looking at?" I ask flatly. I try to sound cool, calm, aloof, like Aria.

"I was . . . remembering something," he says. "About how when you are concentrating, the tip of your nose sort of . . . crinkles up."

"Oh." It's a weird thing to say to someone you are

basically ignoring, and I don't know how to respond to it.

Ebb drifts away, and the moment passes, leaving my head full of the mystery of it.

Germ and I are sitting in the main room playing Spit, and Aria is up at the Grand View studying some Portuguese men-of-war floating by, when it happens. I'm trying to smack-talk Germ about my card-playing skills even though I know I'm bound to lose, when Aria makes a strangled, surprised kind of noise, "OH."

She looks back at us, suddenly tense.

"What is it?" I ask.

"You'd better come look," she says, her voice like gravel.

We all head up to the Grand View as Aria watches us gravely. Then she turns and points to tiny glowing shapes floating here and there around us.

"There," she says. "And there. And there."

I can't quite make them out at first. Whatever they are, they look like small faraway fish—only they *drift through the water* rather than swim. More and more come into view as they come closer to Chompy. There must be hundreds of them.

"What are they?"

"Bottles," Aria says after a moment.

And I see now, upon closer inspection, she's right—the shapes are floating, green glass bottles. All with something curled up inside them.

"They're *messages* in bottles," Aria says. "And I'll bet you anything they all carry the same message."

"Why?" Germ looks up at her. "Why do you think that?"

She taps the air where one of the bottles appears, and we get a zoomed-in closer look. "See? They're all addressed to Rosie, in the same hand."

Sure enough, the closer she zooms (I didn't even know zooming was possible), the easier I can make out the words: *Rosie Oaks, c/o the Time Whale She Rides On*. I recognize the writing from the back of Wolf's photo. It belongs to the Time Witch.

"She must have sent out hundreds of thousands of them, floating through this part of the ocean, hoping one would reach you," Aria says. "Chompy, can you swallow one?" she asks. "And bring it on board?"

A few moments pass as we get closer and closer to one of the floating bottles. There is a slight intake of water, trickling in through the entrance at Chompy's mouth. And then the water gets siphoned back out again through the clever little drains along the edges of the rug, and all that's left behind is one old-looking green glass bottle with a piece of paper clearly rolled up inside.

I snatch it up, but then Germ takes it out of my hands, gently. It's like she's anticipated that whatever's inside is going to hurt me.

Germ fiddles with the cork for a moment, which is so wedged into the top of the bottle that it's almost impossible to pry out, but finally she gets it free.

She unrolls the paper carefully but quickly, and—as she holds it flat—her eyes skim its surface.

Germ goes pale. She looks at me.

She doesn't seem to be able to read it out loud, because she hands it to me silently, looking pained. And I read it instead.

Greetings and salutations, witch hunter!

Dropping a line to ask you how Helike is this time of year. I'll bet it's lovely! I'd come to see you there, but the truth is, it would make our game end rather too quickly, don't you think? I had really hoped you'd be more of a challenge than this, my dear. I thought I'd explained to you how terribly bored I am. I'll give

you one more chance to entertain me.
Incidentally, your brother is well.
He can't send his regards because he doesn't know that you exist. Just today I explained to him that in twenty days, I'll have to take all his years away until he is . . . no more. You can imagine how distressed he was by this news, given that he is not aware there's a soul on Earth who wants to save him. But I feel it only fair to apprise him of the inevitable. Particularly because your attempts to defy me have been so paltry thus far.
It's a shame. Had you never attempted to come after him, had you ignored my game, I suppose I would have forgotten about him altogether and let him at least live out his life. But things take some unexpected turns sometimes after all. I wish it happened more often.

All good wishes,
The Time Witch

The horror creeps over me in inches. When it reaches my knees, I feel them turn to jelly.

"She's going to take all his years away!" Germ tells Aria and Ebb. "Until they're gone. Until . . . he's gone." Ebb meets my eyes, and he looks so stricken that for once it's like he knows me again, and cares. Perched on the coffee table, Little One trembles and begins to chirp frantically. She sounds as desperately wounded and terrified as I feel.

Aria takes the letter, reads it swiftly, then crumples it up and tosses it to the ground. "Don't you believe that, Rosie. She's enraged. You've slipped her traps so far—the hummingbirds, the pirates," she says. "You've worried her, that's why she sent this letter—to intimidate you. Don't let her make you think anything else."

My eyes are drawn to my photo of Wolf again, taped on the wall. How lost he must be, how alone. He doesn't even know about me! He should be home having a normal life. He should be going to school and playing in the yard. And the world should be *good* for him. In the world my brother deserves, witches don't exist. And now, by setting out to save him, I've put him in more danger than ever.

But this doesn't make me angry at myself.

It makes me angry at the witches.

I feel the fear turn into something hard and steely inside me. I see it in Little One too, as she glints and gleams like blue, glowing steel. I forget about the future. I forget about the dark web being woven through the world. I only want to tear every witch limb from limb until my brother is safe.

I look to Ebb. "I'm in," I say. "For the plan. When do we start?"

For a moment no one speaks. Germ closes her eyes. She's doing ESP, but whatever she's trying to communicate to our whale, it's not working.

"Chompy?" Aria finally says, taking control. "We need to find a witch. Any witch."

We hear a howl of whale song. And then singing. Beautiful, haunting singing.

"What's he doing?" Ebb asks out loud.

"He's calling out to the other time whales. Asking where they are."

The haunting sound is all around us for several minutes. And then silence. The timeless ocean, so far from the tumult and change of the world above, stays quiet.

"They're not answering," I whisper.

"Maybe they're too far away," Germ says.

And then there's a faint sound, so faint that it seems

almost imaginary. Somewhere far across the ocean, someone is answering back.

Chompy is perfectly still for a few moments, as if listening. And then there is a tilt and a swish of the room as he rises and sets himself in motion.

I find, now that I've made my choice, I can't wait to start.

The witches have stolen so much from the world: memories, love and connection, my only brother.

I grip my hand around my *Lumos* flashlight, and watch the monitor scroll and toggle and swirl across a vast map of the sea. I don't care where I have to go, as long as I find them.

Now we start stealing from them.

The dark moon is back, and Annabelle Oaks is busy. For the third day in a row, her nightly companion has stayed home. Elaine's other children are missing her, she says. "They're teenagers," she pointed out three nights ago, the bags under her eyes darker than ever, "but they're here, and they need their mother too."

With Germ's mother gone, the ghosts demand all of Annabelle's attention. They tell her their troubles, and she listens, consoles them about lost friends, and friends who have moved

Beyond. She advises them on how to make their graves more inviting. She reads to them and changes the TV to their favorite late-night shows. She paints their portraits.

She cares about these ghosts. But whenever they allow her a moment to herself, she paces, frets, walks the stairs up and down, up and down, all through the long November nights. She can't eat and her body has become willowy, too thin. It's been a month since she saw the strange witch in her yard. Will she come back, now that the moon is dim? Annabelle fears such a return, but she also longs for it.

What does the witch know of Rosie, and how? Why did she come? To warn her, or taunt her? Did she come to curse her? Did she come to help? Annabelle goes to the window for the thousandth time of the night, to watch the sea. It's almost dawn, and she is on the verge of giving up for the night. Once the sun rises, there's no chance the witch will appear.

And then the wind begins to blow, and the hair on the back of Annabelle's neck stands up. A family of squirrels scurries up the side of the house and into the attic for shelter. The trees shiver. The ghosts dart out through the walls in a rush and zip across the yard to the woods. Annabelle's heart leaps as if it has touched an electric wire.

One moment the witch is not there, and the next moment, she is.

This time, she's closer—halfway across the yard—and illuminated by the dim light of the windows shining onto the lawn. She has a dark mole at the side of her mouth, and purple eyelids that match her dress. This time, iridescent white cats, all wearing sparkling purple collars, saunter around the grass that surrounds her, brushing lazily against her ankles.

Annabelle realizes, with a shiver, that she knows *this witch, or stories of her. She was almost killed once, the story goes, trapped inland by a hunter and almost burned to death by the moon. According to the tales, a hundred years old at least, some mysterious circumstance led to her escape.*

Convenia is her name.

When she sees that Annabelle has spotted her, the witch turns toward the footpath that leads down to the ocean along the side of the cliffs. She walks it for a way, then looks back, waiting. She does this twice.

She wants *to be followed.*

Annabelle takes a shuddering breath, steeling herself. She turns to her bed and kneels beside it, and digs from underneath it a bundle of disused arrows, a dusty bow—her weapon, useless for years. But because she can't imagine walking into danger without these things, she takes them on her way out.

When a witch has news of your daughter, even if she's

luring you to your death, you have no choice but to go.

On the beach at the bottom of the path, Convenia is waiting for her. Annabelle steps softly onto the sand. She cradles her arrows in her arms but doesn't try to use them. She waits to be cursed, drowned, killed . . . but she also waits with hope.

Convenia reaches underneath the collar of her dress, untucking an obscured silver whistle, and blows on it.

And then, something moves in the water near the shore.

The round, foaming eddy of a surfacing, speckled whale.

The whale opens its mouth. Convenia watches Annabelle, an invitation in her eyes.

It might be doom. But it also might be Annabelle's only chance to reach what's more precious to her than life.

She walks into the mouth of the whale, and the witch follows her in.

In another moment, they vanish beneath the waves.

Chapter 10

April 5, 1692. 7 p.m. Salem, Massachusetts.

That's the date and time and place that have appeared on Chompy's floating screen overnight. We are standing in the dimness of the Grand View, our faces bathed in blue light.

"Isn't it weird that it's Salem?" Germ muses as we watch the tiny hologram Chompy make its way across the spiral. Beneath our feet, the real Chompy's belly is growling; wherever we are, there aren't much krill. "That's the time of the Salem witch trials. But I thought the Salem witches weren't real. Do you think our teachers were wrong about that?"

"I guess so," I say. But really, I don't know. We learned about the Salem witch trials in fifth grade, but to be honest, I spent a lot of that year staring out the window, imagining the squirrels outside wanted me to be their forest queen.

I remember the basics that Mr. Dubois told us back then, but only vaguely: that the Salem witches weren't r*eal* witches, just *people* who acted a little bit weird or different. And that people sometimes got scared of *weird* or *different*, so they imprisoned them, or worse. (I remember thinking I'd have been in trouble if I'd lived in the 1690s, since I can act pretty weird and different myself sometimes.)

But maybe Mr. Dubois was wrong. After all, I'm pretty sure he didn't think ghosts and magic and moon goddesses were real either. So in general he was kind of off the mark.

"Maybe they're all there, already caught," Germ says hopefully, "and we can swoop in and take *all* their hearts while they're in jail."

The map shows Chompy moving us through a place where New York and 1981 intersect, moving further and further back in time. As we curve past New Jersey, Germ says, to no one in particular, "My grammie says the 1980s never really ended in Jersey." Aria re-tucks her bun and nibbles on something she calls truffle cheese, giving Germ her patented *What are you talking about* look.

I glance over at Ebb, who lingers near his dusty bedroom space, dim and brooding. He doesn't like that we're going to steal from witches without him; I think he's worried for us, though he'd never say it . . . at least not to me.

But then I notice, looking behind him, that Chompy has provided two photos on his nightstand: one grainy black-and-white one of his dead parents—kind-looking people with love in their eyes, his mom blond and light-eyed and his dad dark-haired and bearded with deeply tan skin. And then, weirdly, a picture of me—as a silhouette in my window back home, waving. And then Ebb notices me noticing. He startles, and frowns, and shakes his head slightly. A moment later, the picture vanishes as if he wished Chompy would take it away.

At that same moment, the familiar whooshing of Chompy's tail slows; the bubbling hum of him moving swiftly through the water goes quiet. We've arrived.

"Dim yourself," Aria says to me as we hurry to our room to grab our things. Behind us, Chompy's mouth cracks open, the front wall rising. "Get ready." We grab three knapsacks we've packed with food, sleeping bags, and water. In my mind, I turn the volume down on my sight—something I've been practicing for days. I wrap my hands around my hourglass, and watch the sand start to trickle.

Here we go.

Cold ocean water floods in and laps at our feet as we take in the view of a serene, rocky beach. A grassy green field lies beyond it, and the smell of wood fires wafts through the air. As Chompy's map indicated, it's evening, the sun just sinking toward the horizon.

"We'll be fine," Aria says, but I can tell she's as nervous as we are. One by one, we step into knee-deep water and trudge ashore.

Watching the sky for hummingbirds, Aria heads straight for the edge of the woods to a path that leads into the forest. She crouches, staring at a spot on the ground, and motions us closer to look at it too. At first I think it's only a shadowy blotch, a trick of the light. But then I see it's not a shadow at all. The closer I look, the more clearly I see the vaguest outline of a shoe.

"Whoa," Germ says. "Creepy."

I would have never noticed it on my own, but now that Aria has drawn my attention to the footprint, I see them evenly spaced up ahead along the path, like the barest hint of shadows. I reach out to touch the one in front of me, and my fingers feel immediately cold.

"Witches leave footprints wherever they walk," Aria explains. "You can even see them in daytime, once you're really paying attention. It's the absence of light that makes them stand out. A regular shadow can be beautiful, but a witch footprint looks . . . empty. Like you're staring into nothing."

"I've never even noticed them," I say, frustrated with my lack of hunting abilities.

I expect Aria to give me one of her superior looks, but she softens a little. "Well, obviously you need the *sight* to see them, but even after you get it, they're very subtle." She pats my shoulder kindly. "Anyway, Clara always said that if you noticed all the invisible things in the world—ALL the fabric at once—you'd go mad. You've got to adapt a little at a time."

"Well, I sure could have used it when I was trying to find the Memory Thief," I say.

"Butter late than never," Germ says. It's a random thing we like to say whenever we add butter to our pancakes after sleepovers; for some reason it cracks us up. Aria glances at Germ with an unimpressed look, then turns back to the path.

"Why would she land so far up the shore from town?" Aria wonders aloud, glancing around for any signs of human life. "I suppose she wanted to curse people living in the outskirts along the way."

We keep the trail of footprints as our eerie marker as we forge into the woods, the witch's path running a few hundred yards from the ocean, but parallel to it. We have no idea what witch we're following or if she or he knows we're coming. As the sky darkens, Little One lights our way. I check my hourglass often to look at the sand trickling down, watching the glowing red number twenty fade as the evening wears on. After a while, we sit on a fallen log to eat and rest. But we don't linger long.

By full nightfall we can hear the distant sound of children playing and smell chimney smoke in the air. The magical world is coming alive for the night, and we soon pass a ghost in a beautiful suede beaded robe sitting on a log, making something intricate out of wood. He looks at us for a moment and then gets back to what he's doing, unconcerned. Ghosts, of course, can see everything, sight or not.

Eventually we pass a farmhouse with warmly lit windows. A man stands in the front yard, picking a cabbage for his dinner. Beside him, a shaggy dog sniffs the air and glares at us, barking. The man follows the dog's gaze, his eyes brushing right past us as we stand frozen in place. Then he returns to his work. Unlike the ghosts, he doesn't see us—not even a bit. If he's cursed, I can't see any evidence of it.

We eat a late dinner of beef jerky and beans, resting our legs but not for long. Other than a ghostly couple who drift through our campfire at one point (they nod to us but are too deep in conversation with each other to slow down), we are alone. It's the night before dark moon, so only a waning crescent of moonlight rises above, with only the tiniest hint of a ladder dangling from its side.

I feel a moment's sadness that the Moon Goddess seems more unreachable than ever, though around the moon the beauty of the Beyond has begun to sparkle. Cloud shepherds move through the air far above, and Aria lets out a longing sigh.

"It's nice to see the sky the way it's supposed to be," she says softly. "By the time I was born, it was already dim."

By morning, we realize that we'll need to sleep if we are going to sustain ourselves. We find a tucked-away glade well off the witch's path and close our eyes for a few hours before resuming midday. The deeper we get into civilization, the more clear it becomes that, to everyone we pass, we are invisible. Kids traipsing through the forest ignore us; women carrying bundles of wood walk right past us. Only animals and ghosts know of our presence, squirrels scurrying out of our way, dogs perking their ears toward us. We eat under the canopy of an oak tree.

"This must be what it's like to be a spirit floating around," I say to Germ. "We're here, but we're not. We're real, but we don't belong."

I think about it as we walk, Aria keeping careful track of the witch's path as we go: the people we see along our way are doing things they haven't actually done for hundreds of years, living lives that ended long before I was born.

And yet all these lost moments are still happening, thanks to the Sea of Always. It makes me think, with a pang, about my dad. He died, but also, in the past, I guess he's not dead at all. Somewhere he's alive and doing the same things he used to do, on and on forever. If only I could find him in time, I could see the little things no one can really tell you: what his face looks like when he laughs, what his voice sounds like, how he smells. Those are the kinds of things you want to know about a dad you've never met.

"Rosie!" Aria whispers.

Daydreaming. I turn my inner volume down the best I can and look around me. It's dusk again, and I see that while my mind's been somewhere else, we've arrived at the edge of Salem. Plain but pretty brick buildings line up in criss-crossing rows ahead of us, and doorways flicker with lantern light. We see draft horses tied to posts, dimmed stores, one clergyman hurrying toward what looks like a courthouse. But that's not why Aria has grabbed my attention.

There's a creature waddling across the road in front of us. It's a chameleon, green and bright . . . and totally out of place in Massachusetts. The evening is just dark enough for us to see its ghostly glow. My heart thuds faster; there's no mistaking the iridescent sparkle of a witch's familiar. The creature ignores us completely, which means that, at least, the dimming is working.

I try to remember which witch chameleons belong to. I should know, since I've read *The Witch Hunter's Guide* about a million times. But in my nervousness, the witch's name and face elude me. Even Aria appears to be drawing a blank.

The creature scurries to the edge of the road and into the grass. It's joined by two more at the top of a rise, and then they disappear across the field.

"There should be more people in town. Where is everyone?" Germ says nervously.

"I don't know," Aria says, "but those chameleons were on a mission."

We stare in the direction the chameleons went. The witch's footprints lead the opposite way, through town and out the other side. But it feels like, to find the witch, we should follow her pets. At least, that's what worked with the Memory Thief. I look at my hourglass anxiously. The number twenty has faded completely, and the number nineteen is now in its place. A little over twenty-four hours have passed since we landed. We don't have time for mistakes.

"Let's follow those chameleons to see where they're headed," I say. "Only for a few minutes."

We are luckier than we expect. We find the missing people, *and the witch*, all gathered at the edge of a river not five minutes later.

The witch has been captured, and is about to be drowned.

Completely unnoticed, we slip up to the back of a gaggle of people gathered at the water's edge. A severe man wearing a sour, wrinkled expression and a white curled wig, some kind of magistrate maybe (I do remember the word "magistrate" from Mr. Dubois), stands at the front of the crowd. There are torches planted in the dirt on either side of him to illuminate the scene. I gasp as I see a chameleon climb out of his sleeve and slither down his leg and away, glowing with whatever it's stolen from him. *He's been cursed already,* I realize.

The crowd jostles a little, and finally I see that the person at the center of all the attention is not the man in the wig, but a small, wild-haired woman to his left. She's standing at the river's edge, flanked by two men holding her arms, and glaring back at the crowd defiantly.

The man in the wig gestures at her, and speaks loudly. I recognize the look on his face as he does. It's the look my mother used to wear under her curse, like he is here, but also far away.

"Gentlefolk, we are here tonight to carry out the sentence passed upon this avowed witch, based upon the testimony of our good citizens in this year of our Lord 1692. We hereby attest that this witch has cursed our crops and caused them to fail, challenged the magistrates in a most blasphemous manner, and struck terror into the hearts of the God-fearing citizens of this town."

The crowd begins to murmur as I study the woman, whose defiant expression is dissolving into fear. She doesn't match any of the drawings in my book; she's pale, and small, wild-haired, and twitchy. She doesn't look so different from *me*, and she certainly doesn't look scary. Then again, my mother was drawing from rumors and stories. Maybe she missed this witch, or didn't get her right.

In the murmurs around me, I can tell that all are in agreement that the woman before them is evil. But amongst the noise and motion, I do notice an old man standing at the outside of the crowd, silent and set apart—looking disgusted with his neighbors. For a moment, I could swear there's something special about him, something particularly alert and awake.

As the judge continues, I see more chameleons—slithering around under the skirts of women around me, between people's feet, out from under robes and coats. Aria and I look at each other nervously. For one thing, we don't want the creatures to notice us. For another, it's clear that it's not just the magistrate but most of the people around us who've been witch-touched and cursed. We're surrounded by them.

"Gentlefolk," the judge says again. "I have listened with care to your accusations. And we have come here to mete out the punishment that is required."

I watch the woman's face shudder at these words. And suddenly it comes back to me who chameleons belong to.

Hypocriffa. She's the sixth witch in the *Guide.* I remember her clearly now: a woman with sewn-up ears and a finger poised before her lips. And suddenly I know what's happening.

History was wrong about witches, but not in the way I thought. There *were* witches in Salem, but they weren't the ones who got drowned. *And this woman is no witch.*

"Martha Parker," the judge goes on, "you hereby stand convicted of witchcraft. You shall now face trial by water. If you drown, you will die the death of the innocent. If you float, we will know for certain that you're a witch."

The woman, Martha, slumps and lets out a moan.

"I never understood the logic there," Germ whispers.

"They're lying! They're *all* lying!" I whisper, panicked. Aria reaches out an arm to settle me. "*They're* the ones doing something terrible, not her! Only, they don't know it. They're all cursed."

The injustice of it panics me. They can't drown this woman. They can't!

Germ, who never needs to be convinced to take me at my word, immediately starts to jostle forward, ready to fight, ready to save Martha Parker. She's ready to make a one-girl charge at the crowd, despite being both invisible and weaponless. I draw Little One out of my pocket. Aria grabs our sleeves and pulls us both still.

"Absolutely not!" she hisses. "If we change this woman's fate, the Time Witch will hear the change *immediately*. She'll come back in time and trap us *immediately*. And all will be lost. Everything. Not to mention, we're not supposed to tamper with the human past."

Germ gets red. She looks to Aria, uncertain.

"I want to help too," Aria whispers. "But the best way to help people . . . *all* people," she continues, "is to destroy *all* the witches. All at once. Like we've planned. This woman is lost to us. We have to find the witch who's laid this curse, the one who sent the chameleons in the first place. She's not here, and"—she nods at the hourglass at my neck, where the number nineteen has already started to fade from the top down—"we're losing valuable time. We've got to go."

In a moment, Aria has us moving away. She's tugging us along by our sleeves, while we resist less and less. I know she's right, but I can't help looking over my shoulder at the crowd behind us, horrified.

And because I'm looking back, I notice one curious thing as we hurry away. I see the old man, the one who *seemed* so alert and awake, moving away from the crowd quietly. He makes his way to the trees at the edge of the water, as if he doesn't want to be noticed—though I can't understand why. All I can see is that, even though he looks old and frail and not like any kind of magical person at all, he leaves a silver glow, faint and subtle like moonlight, along the ground behind him as he walks. It disappears quickly, and it's so dark, I think I must have imagined it. But it gives me a strange kind of hope for the woman by the river, for no reason I can explain.

The last I see of the crowd or anyone else is the man walking into the woods at the water's edge. And then he slips out of my sight.

CHAPTER 11

Back in town, we reconnect to the witch's trail and follow it down the main avenue into the forest at the other edge of Salem, weaving onto the outskirts of the town and beyond, moving inland and away from the sea. This forest is deeper, thicker, full of the calls of owls and the sounds of unseen animals scrabbling through the trees. The night of dark moon has arrived, and Little One lights our way in the moonless dark. Our legs ache.

Here the footprints—even now they can be distinguished by their absolute foot-shaped emptiness—come closer together, as if the witch were tiring, taking smaller steps. As we walk, my heart stays with the woman we've left behind and the cruelty of the people around her. I feel terrible leaving her.

A few more hours pass before our trail turns through a fence into a small yard, surrounded by trees and full of thick and impossible brambles. We slow, holding our breath as we trail the footprints to one small, narrow opening in the thorns. After squeezing in and through them, careful not to rustle them for fear of being noticed, we emerge to find a tiny clearing and a brick cottage with untamed roses growing all around it.

A few chameleons squeeze under the gap at the threshold of the front door. I reach for my flashlight and clutch it tightly in my pocket. Looking at each other, eyes wide, we tiptoe slowly up to the windows and peer inside. And gasp.

The inside of the house is old and decrepit, with walls half-eaten away by termites, soot-covered broken furniture, a bed so crooked that the yellowed mattress has been moved to the floor. And all of it—every wall, every floorboard, every piece of furniture—is covered with chameleons. Chameleons crawling on the empty iron stove, slithering through the rotting hay strewn across the floor.

The witch sits in the middle, on a crooked wooden bench, her profile to us.

She is smiling to herself, plump and beautiful and contented as she sits on her bench in a bright turquoise dress. But her ears are sewn shut. And there is a steely set to her smile, as if the moment she were to stop smiling, she would start screaming in rage. I know, from my mom's description of her and from her even for a moment, that she is not a *listener* like Ebb, trying to hear and understand the whispers of the world. Hypocriffa, I remember, is the opposite of that. She steals whatever it is that lets us put ourselves in other people's shoes, the recognition of one soul from another. And in the absence of that, she leaves an empty opening for distrust.

The chameleons crawl onto her lap like a cozy blanket and around her feet like slippers, and something curious happens as they do. As they move over and around her, their breaths rise up—visible, like dandelion puffs floating in the air, only made of the same dark emptiness as the footprints we've been following.

The breath fluff is like a cotton candy of nothingness—not the beautiful color of crows or still black nights with stars, but something instead that seems to swallow light and devour it.

"What's happening?" I whisper. I don't think there's much chance of a witch whose ears are sewn shut hearing us, especially when we're on the other side of a wall. But I keep my voice very low just in case.

"It's like," Aria speculates uncertainly, "whatever they're stealing, they're breathing out the emptiness of witches—something its opposite. Like how people breathe in oxygen and breathe out carbon dioxide." But she looks as confused as I feel. When *Aria* looks confused, it makes me nervous.

The witch waves her hands above the creatures, collecting the darkness in her fingers. She plays with it a bit—fluffing and smushing and expanding it. And then she tucks it, handful by handful, into a rough-hewn basket with a lid, like a sewing basket. She then pulls a long, thin wooden contraption out of her sleeve, unfolds it, and rests it on the ground—a spinning wheel. From her bench, she leans over the wheel and begins to spin the tufts into long, dark yarn, pumping the spinner into motion with her foot, letting each long thread of tufty fluff through her fingers slowly as she pulls it out of the basket.

"I always heard witches described as crafty, but I didn't know they meant, like, *crafts*," Germ whispers. Aria blinks at her. "I feel bad for the chameleons, though," she adds. "She took their breath."

"Germ." I level my gaze at her. "They are *literally* pure evil." Aria doesn't understand—like I do—that Germ's love for everything and everyone is her greatest weakness. A witch who steals people's sympathy for each other is pretty much Germ's opposite in every way.

"How are we going to steal her heart if she's surrounded by, like, nine hundred guards?" I whisper. "We don't even know where the heart is." I'm looking around the room, but it's so disheveled that it's hard to tell where the furniture is, much less a heart.

And then, I finally see something that reminds me of Ebb's description. Aria nudges me and points to it at the exact same time. It's a small but heavy-looking metal box, rusted and covered in soot like it's been through a few fires. It sits beside the yellowed mattress, as if it's important enough to keep close but not quite important enough to take good care of. Just as Ebb said, it's clearly a neglected appendage. We're betting the world on it being, also, a *necessary* appendage. It lies only a few feet across the littered floor, and yet it may as well be miles away, the room is so packed with familiars.

I look at Aria. "Any chance you can do something?" I ask.

She shakes her head, and for a moment her eyes flare

with something—anger or sorrow or both. "In the old days, I could have sung something, put the chameleons to sleep, laid a song over them like a blanket. Now . . ." She shakes her head again. "Anyway, none of us can do *anything* till she sleeps."

The witch goes on spinning, and we stay crouched by the window, waiting. I toggle back and forth between obsessively watching the sand slide through my hourglass and trying to think of what to do.

Finally, somewhere close to dawn, the witch leans back in her chair, drowsy. She stands, walks to the doorway, and leaves the ball of yarn she's made on the threshold outside the door, as we duck back farther behind a bush, watching.

Then she walks to her yellowed mattress and lies down on it, and goes still immediately. Germ may sleep the sleep of the untroubled, but this witch sleeps the deathlike sleep of someone who has no conscience at all.

I turn my flashlight on. Little One sits there amongst the twigs and dried leaves at my feet, waiting for my command. But what *is* my command? How do I retrieve a heart from a box surrounded by hundreds of reptiles who will wake the witch on sight of me?

Aria and Germ stare at me. "Okay, Rosie," Aria says.

"Okay what?"

"You gotta . . . do whatever it is you do."

"There's no way those chameleons won't see Little One," I say. In the Memory Thief's cave, I had to *fight*, but I didn't have to go *unnoticed*. This is a whole different thing.

"Can you please *try* your weapon?" I ask Aria sheepishly.

Aria gives me a flat look. "You know I'd knock the whole house down and half of Salem. Not much of a secret."

I think quietly, trying to ignore that we are losing time. I have flashbacks to Little One being pulled out of the sky by the horde of hummingbirds at Aria's island, so helpless. Self-doubt turns my throat dry.

Germ looks at me, flushed. "Maybe you could shrink her into a *tiny* bird, so they don't notice her."

"But she'd still have to carry the heart past them," I say.

They both stare at me. "No pressure, Rosie, take your time," Aria says sarcastically, while her eyes bulge out at me in urgency. We sit there and sit there and sit there, staring at each other. I wish I were alone to think. People watching me, even Aria and Germ in this case, are my kryptonite.

And then, because I can't take any more of the staring, I close my eyes. I try to forget there's a witch on the other side of the wall that could destroy my chance of ever saving Wolf. I try to imagine I'm alone . . . alone and safe to dream. I tighten my hands around my *Lumos* flashlight. I try to remember where Little One came from and why: a story to devour all the cruelty of witch darkness. I wanted to fight back against something too big for me to win against.

"Don't let your sight glow too brightly," Germ whispers. But if I'm glowing like a beacon that witches can see, for now I can't help it. I can't dim myself and imagine at the same time.

I think how a witch like Hypocriffa—who steals people's sympathy—tells only one story, a story that's big and simple and loud: *distrust, fear, judge.* That's the story people were telling, at the water's edge, condemning that woman they thought was a witch.

And then I think of the woman's innocence, and it wrenches at my guts how I couldn't help her. I think about how a truthful story is not loud or simple at all, how a real story lays small and slight things along a path you have to be curious enough to look for. It reminds me of a cricket: a cricket is so tiny, but its little song can keep a person up all night. The true things of the world seem kind of like that.

Once, I think, *a cricket hopped near the ear of a dragon*, *to sing about what was quiet and real. The dragon thought the cricket was no match for him. He swatted, and roared, and breathed fire to quench the creature's tiny song. But the cricket—being so small—hid in crevices, ducked behind rocks, and kept singing. It drove the dragon so wild, singing day and night, that in trying to set it on fire in a rage, the dragon set himself on fire instead. And the loud, blustering giant burned into ash.*

It makes me feel a little better, telling myself this story. Even if it doesn't—

"Rosie," Germ whispers, touching my arm. "Um. I think you broke Little One."

I open my eyes. And lose my breath.

Standing on the ground in front of me, Little One is not Little One anymore. Or at least, not the Little One I know. I only recognize her by her glow, and the bond between us that's tied around my heart, but she is no longer a bluebird at all.

She's a cricket.

I look at her in shock. "She doesn't *have* to be a bluebird?" I whisper, even more surprised than Germ and Aria, whose mouths are hanging open. "She can be *other* things?"

"She's *your* weapon," Aria says in wonder. "And you are truly weird. I love it."

I'm trying to think of what it really means, that Little

One can shape-shift. Could I turn her into other animals? What are the rules?

"But, Rosie," Germ says, squinting in the pained way she does when she gives me bad news, "what can a cricket do? This does *not* solve our problem."

But Aria seems to get it before both of us, because her eyes are twinkling.

"Well, what do chameleons eat?" she asks.

And I see it, that without even completely thinking about it, I've made Little One the juiciest, most delicious cricket a reptile could ever see. And then I realize why.

"She's not going to go in and sneak in past them," I say. "She's going to *lure them out*."

I stare at this new version of Little One, grasping how much I don't know about my witch weapon and what she's capable of, even after all this time. And then I slowly lift my flashlight and shine it at the bottom of the cottage's front door, my heart in my throat.

"Be careful," I say to her, but she ignores me, like some fearless part of my soul. The cricket version of Little One hops under the crack under the door. And we watch through the window as, suddenly, she has the attention of every chameleon in the room.

It only takes a few moments. The chameleons all look

in her direction, and their tongues begin to dart quickly out of their mouths, tantalized. Little One is quicker, and hops back out under the door again. We watch in relief as the chameleons follow, squiggling out through the small crack after her. Every single chameleon in the room jockeys to be the next to clamber outside after its prey.

Breathless, I shine Little One toward the woods, worried for her. We watch in awe as the multitude of chameleons follows, numerous and as squiggly as worms, down the path and around a curve. The moment they are out of sight, Germ stands abruptly.

"I'm going in," she says.

"Germ," I hiss. But Germ slips up to the door before Aria or I can stop her. She is bolder than she is reasonable. And while Germ generally has no "inside voice," she is also incredibly graceful, and she moves through the room like a cat burglar. We watch her through the window as the witch sleeps, as still as a corpse.

Germ crosses the room to the metal box, gently lifts the lid, and stares at what's inside with a shuddering, disgusted look on her face. She puts the thing into a small cloth sack (provided by Chompy, I suppose) she pulls from her knapsack, and goes to put the lid back on, but she is moving so quickly, with such nervousness, that she knocks the box over. The lid makes a clatter even we can hear from outside. Germ is stock-still, staring at the witch.

Hypocriffa doesn't budge.

Then I feel a tug at my sleeve. Aria draws my attention to the woods. My stomach churns.

The chameleons have given up. They've cleared the bend in the path and are headed back toward the cottage. I see in the distance the tiny glow of Little One behind them, hopping wildly and trying to get their attention again. Without success.

I tap on the window gently, so that Germ looks over as she's just tightening the sack closed. I wave for her to hurry out, but she thinks I'm giving her the thumbs-up. Her mouth widens in a huge, goofy grin, and she gives me the thumbs-up back. Watching the chameleons close in across the grass, an iridescent army moving like water, I begin to gesture frantically.

Finally Germ seems to get what I'm communicating. Her eyes widen in panic, looking toward the door.

She rushes toward the window on tiptoes and slides it open as quietly as she can. Then, like a contortionist, she slips in and out and through, scooping her body sideways.

As she slides out with a hiss and shuts the window with a creak, the witch startles. She sits up, gazing around the floor with sharp turquoise eyes. The chameleons are filtering back into the room under her gaze, curling and uncurling their tails, wiggling as they walk. We duck, the sack clutched close to Germ's heaving ribs as she tries to catch her breath. Can the witch sense us out here in the dark?

We wait for the witch to come to the window, for an explosion of chameleons to burst out through the door. But nothing. I slowly lift my head up, and peer back inside. Hypocriffa has gone back to sleep.

Germ slides the sack into my hands.

My palms drop under its weight. Whatever's in it, it's heavy, wet, and like Jell-O. I stuff it into my coat pocket, along with my flashlight—and the cricket version of Little One disappears.

I begin to stand, but Aria grabs my wrist and yanks me back down. Crouching again, I follow her eyes.

A figure is approaching, a person of some sort, and the closer they get, the more troubled I feel. Who would be coming, in the middle of the night, to find a witch? It's only when he rounds the bend that we see for certain, the answer is: another witch.

This time, I know exactly who this one is. Dread. He looks very much like my mother's drawing in the *Guide*—tall and gaunt, with bottomless eyes glinting in the dark.

A hyena follows behind him, luminescent, nipping at his heels—though he takes no notice. I remember that, in the *Guide*, I always thought he was with a wolf, but either the book got it wrong or I did. The hyena somehow looks much worse.

Dread walks up to Hypocriffa's door and takes the ball of yarn from where she's placed it on the threshold. He tucks it into his sleeve and, without even pausing, turns and walks back into the woods.

We wait for several minutes, hoping that he's really gone. And then we emerge from the bushes.

"Why would he be here?" I whisper to Aria. "What would he want with a ball of that yarn?"

"I don't know," Aria says, looking as troubled and bewildered as I am. "But I don't think we'll be getting his heart tonight." I look in the direction Dread has gone. I fear the day we'll have to steal from him, but for now, I think Aria's right. We're exhausted, and we need to get a handle on exactly what it is we've stolen.

"We're *hours* behind schedule," Aria adds. "It'll take less time than coming, but still probably all day and most of the night to get back to Chompy."

Once we're sure Dread is gone, we sneak on soft feet into the woods, and walk silently until we are a safe distance away from the cottage. It's not until we are making our way seaward, that I really start to breathe again.

Like thieves in the night, we hurry on our long journey back toward the ocean's edge, carrying our strange quarry with us.

CHAPTER 12

Ebb, Aria, Germ, and I are gathered on the shag rug in a circle, looking at the little sickly jiggling sack in my hands. By my hourglass, we've given up two and a half days for this first heart—the blood-red number eighteen is faded almost down to the middle. But we did *steal a heart*. And that's something.

We've already asked Chompy to look for the next whale. He's been calling for an hour into the great blue yonder, but so far, no answers.

"Should we look at it?" I ask, worried what a witch

heart is capable of. Could it bite us, cling to us like a leech? Can it sense we have stolen it? Tell the witches where we are?

"Duh," says Germ, never one to err on the side of caution. "Of course."

My hands shaking a little, I begin to loosen the drawstring on the sack.

Germ grabs the empty Dorito bowl from the table, and I upend the sack so that the heart slides into it, and lands on some crushed orange crumbs.

We stare into the bowl.

The heart is not the kind of heart any real creature would actually have; it is not heart-shaped at all. It's a gleaming red apple.

Wincing, I poke at it, and my finger sinks into its surface, like sinking into Jell-O. Like the witches, it's like it's half-real but half-unreal, there and not there.

Germ reaches out to touch it too. Her touch rolls the apple onto its side, and we all groan. There's a rotten hole on one side, brown and decayed and smelly.

I quickly drape the sack over it, scoop it in, and pull the drawstring tight, and then drop the sack beside me, disgusted. I won't be looking at witch hearts any more than I need to, I decide.

"That seems like the perfect heart for Hypocriffa," Aria says. "Good on the surface, rotten and cruel underneath. Like that judge. Like all those cursed people accusing that woman." We already have *The Witch Hunter's Guide* lying open on the floor beside us. Next to the picture of Hypocriffa my mother drew are some words she jotted down in messy handwriting as if following a train of thought: *For those she's cursed, it's easy to make harming others feel right. It's easy to make other people out to be monsters.*

But Hypocriffa's heart raises more questions than it answers. Do all witch hearts look like this . . . not like hearts at all? Is each one different, reflecting the essence of whom they belong to? There is so much about the invisible layers of the world I have yet to learn.

Still, none of those answers matters as long as I can destroy them. And it looks easy enough. Little One has devoured an entire witch—heart, guts, and all. One small rotten apple heart won't be a problem. I only wish I could have her do it right now.

"So chameleon breath was being spun into yarn?" Ebb asks. He still won't meet my eyes, though he looked like he was about to faint with relief when we reached Chompy a few minutes ago.

We've filled him in on most of what happened since

we left him, but we're also still figuring it out ourselves—the dark, empty tufts of breath Hypocriffa was spinning at her wheel, and the strange appearance of the second witch, Dread. Ebb flickers as we talk. I think worry for us has drained him a bit.

"I don't know," I say. "But there's something about that yarn that's important. Otherwise why would another witch come to collect it?"

My imagination goes wild wondering what the answer is. Are they knitting a rope ladder to the moon? Or a literal web? What does it have to do with the dark void left by witch footprints? Still, the others don't seem as fixated on the yarn as I am. Germ always says I let my imagination run away with me.

"The awful Salem judge said this ridiculous thing about how witches float," Germ tells Ebb, interrupting my thoughts.

"Well, they've got it mixed around," Aria offers matter-of-factly. "Witches can't swim. Even though they're always traveling the Sea of Always. Clara told me that; she thought it was ironic."

This gets our attention. We all blink at her for a moment. "We could drown *them*!" Germ suddenly exclaims. "Let's drown them all instead of stealing their hearts."

Ebb and I exchange a smirk; we know Germ couldn't drown a fly. But then Ebb remembers he's avoiding me and drops the smirk.

"If you could ever catch one to drown," Aria says bitterly. "Much less nine of them . . . plus the Time Witch."

Germ's shoulders slump.

Aria ignores her disappointment. "But if stealing each heart is as hard as stealing that one was, we don't stand a chance." She looks at me. "We have to be faster, Rosie. I mean," she corrects, seeming to remember she is only helping to get her voucher, "*you* need to be faster."

I swallow. "Next time will be easier," I say. "Next time I'll know what to do. I'll know I can change Little One."

We all look at each other, uncertain.

"What do *I* know?" Germ murmurs, to no one in particular, with disappointment and maybe a tiny bit of longing. "I'm only the assistant."

It's a little bit of a to-do, deciding where to keep the dark heart of one of the most sinister creatures in the universe. Aria suggests we each take turns sleeping with it, and Germ is certain Chompy will think of something and give us the perfect place for it like he always does. But no padded safe or lockable pirate chest is forthcoming, so I end up putting the heart into my backpack, in the main compartment. (Since I always keep at least one favorite book in the front pocket for good luck. Right now it's *The Snowy Day*, which I've borrowed from my shelf because it always reminds me the world is beautiful.) My rationale is that at least my backpack has a zipper, and surely a witch heart cannot unzip something and escape, considering it has no opposable thumbs.

That night in bed, while Germ and Ebb and Aria are goofing off playing gin rummy in the living room (our card game repertoire is expanding by the day, thanks to Aria), and Ebb is filling the extra time by showing them how to empty people's pockets without them knowing (something he learned from his years of imprisonment with the ghost thief named Steve), I fiddle around with my flashlight, trying to see what else I can turn Little One into. But it's slow going. She occasionally flickers into a cricket again, and once, I get her to be a mosquito, but that's about it. Apparently, I can't transform Little One if my whole heart isn't in it. And that's not easy when I'd rather be playing gin rummy and learning how to pick pockets and not be feeling left out.

I watch them even though I pretend not to. It's clear that Ebb and Germ have picked up their friendship right where they left off; they laugh and joke with each other, discussing over cards the pros and cons of talking to nature. (Sometimes, according to Ebb, trees tell you things you don't want to hear by, say, pointing a branch toward an oncoming storm.) But it's like they're talking about two different things. Ebb wants to learn and understand everything. He's deeply curious about how nature works and how it whispers to us in ways most people don't notice. Germ, on the other hand, just wants to be able to ask Chompy if she can give him a hug.

"Like the other day, I told him via ESP to eat some krill, and he definitely did," she says unconvincingly. Ebb smiles at her affectionately, glowing a little brighter.

Meanwhile, Ebb and Aria are also clearly hitting it off.

On a whim, I decide to channel my inner Aria to see if that changes things. I lower my eyelids in an aloof *I don't care* kind of way and try to walk up to the game of gin rummy with a casual elegance.

Ebb looks up at me, staring for a moment.

"Are you okay?" he says flatly.

"What do you mean?" I ask in what seems to me a cool, aloof voice.

"You're doing something weird with your eyebrows," he says, then turns back to the game.

I slink off and up to the Grand View, restless, worried, and hemmed in all at the same time. I watch the years and miles roll past as Chompy circles the time spiral, waiting for the next call.

I turn my mind to Salem again, my thoughts revolving around the innocent woman by the water. Was she really drowned? I feel so responsible for her. And then it occurs to me: If Chompy can provide anything I need, could he provide me something I need that's also from the past?

"Chompy, do you have any newspapers from Salem, the week of April 5, 1692?" I ask. I'm not sure if, back then, newspapers even existed.

I look up at the monitor, and when I look down again, there's a small newspaper rack attached to the wall at the side of the Grand View. I pull out the one newspaper hanging from the top bar, a browning paper crowded with small black type in heavy square paragraphs.

I flip through the pages gently until I find what I'm looking for.

Woman, Martha Parker, escapes trial by drowning.

My pulse spikes.

I read on, about how Martha Parker was condemned as a witch. About the evening she was scheduled to be drowned. When I get to the next paragraph, I feel a wondering grin stretch across my face: *It's believed she was aided by a man belonging to the seditious and nefarious Witch Freedom Society of Salem. A bounty has been placed on the heads of all individuals involved.*

My heart lifts. The man I saw. It was he who saved her, I am sure of it. But how and why did he leave that misty light behind him?

My thoughts are interrupted by a sudden, haunting sound. It's a low distant hum—beautiful, mournful, a call from somewhere far away.

In another moment, Aria pops up beside me to look at the Grand View. We watch as tiny Chompy's circling comes to a halt and he heads left, cutting across the spiral quickly and surely. By the swish of the water around us, we can tell he is picking up speed.

"It's the next whale," Aria says, "calling out to him. We're on our way."

CHAPTER 13

We are headed to 1952, to a town called Onno on the coast of Nigeria.

As we get close to shore, my heart beating a fast rhythm, an enormous shape swims just in front of us, blocking everything else. It brushes right up against us, and Chompy goes wobbling, knocking us all off our feet.

We watch the Grand View monitor in shock as the shape that's hit us makes itself clear. We see the large black eye of a whale, and then its body as it swims away. We shake, wafted in the current of its tail, and Chompy lets out a cry.

"He's annoyed," Germ says, touching her temples and trying to sound like she is reading Chompy's mind. "I think these two are in a tiff about something. That's what I'm picking up on."

"What would whales even argue about?" Aria scoffs.

"I wonder which witch it belongs to," I say.

At that moment, as Germ's about to hazard an uninformed ESP guess, there's an enormous *whoosh*. Chompy jerks upward in something of a leap, opens his mouth without warning, and just sort of . . . spits us into the open air. I let out a yelp as we fly through the sky, and then land on hard ground, tumbling and groaning.

I sit up, my hip and shoulder aching from the landing.

Out on the water, Ebb stands in Chompy's open mouth, glowing in the darkness and looking as if he's embarrassed by Chompy's bad behavior, and holding up one hand to wave. "Good lu—" he calls out, but he's cut off as Chompy slams his mouth closed and dives.

"Told you he's annoyed," Germ says.

"I don't trust that whale," I say.

After sitting stunned for a moment, we stand and brush ourselves off, dimming ourselves and looking around. I pull out Little One and send her ahead several yards so she can illuminate what's around us.

We're on a slim slice of beach; it's a warm night, and again the tiniest sliver of moon hangs in the sky, with its unreachable hint of a ladder. By its position, Aria reckons it's about three a.m. At the edge of the sand is a field that leads up into rolling green hills that disappear into the black night. It's peaceful, beautiful, inviting, but as our eyes adjust, we also start to see *it*, the trail of shadowy footprints mostly obscured by tall grass, easy to miss or mistake for dips in the ground. A witch has come this way, and the sand in my hourglass is, of course, already falling.

"We've gotta move quickly," I say, "and make up for lost time."

We walk in a tight row into the field before us, looking around for the shadows that mark our trail. There are wild animals in Nigeria, Germ informs us, bigger than anything Maine has to offer. She saw it on *Wild Discovery: Animal Whisperer*. We don't want to meet them, particularly when, even with Little One's light, we can only see a few yards around us. While we've prepared ourselves for witches, we're not prepared for a stampede of elephants.

We walk . . . and walk . . . and walk . . . for hours and

into dawn. Unlike in Salem, there's no sign of a town or people nearby.

Seeing me reach for my hourglass again, Aria stays my hand. "It won't make this go faster," she says.

And it's a good thing I stop obsessing, because a few moments later we come upon a gathering of enormous, living silhouettes in the dark. After a heart-stopping moment of terror, the glow of Little One reveals it is a family of giraffes, staring at us with curiosity from behind the trees.

"Oh!" Germ gasps, jerking to a stop. "I love them soooo much."

For once I have to agree with her. It's magical to come across giraffes in the wild, maybe as magical as witches and ghosts. In another moment, though, I have to nudge her to keep walking. I suppose if we stop and linger at every place we find interesting in this past world, we'll never make it anywhere.

Shortly before dawn, we pass a group of ghosts standing and chatting by a river—all women. But the rest of the morning is uneventful. We rest around lunchtime—lying down for a brief nap under the shade of a tree—and move on as soon as we're rested and fed. We push on for the rest of the afternoon and into evening, snacking but not stopping, trekking long past sunset and into the night. Little One lights our way as another night, this one moonless, descends, our feet weary and our legs aching.

It's getting late, and we're thinking about stopping to rest for a bit, when we come to the rise of a green hill and find, on the other side, a town. From above, it looks like a small gathering of shadows only barely visible in the dark. There are maybe fifty or so modest houses nestled in the valley before us.

The whole place appears to be asleep. But one figure moves from house to house, a white glowing shape wandering the village's edges. If he glanced up the hill now, he'd see us. But he's too focused on what he is doing to look.

The witch is already at work.

We stand frozen in place and watch, afraid to move. Even from here, he is terrifyingly skeletal and all too familiar: *the Griever.*

Words about him from the *Guide* leap out in my memory: blind, mournful, acute hearing. Steals joy.

He has a pale white, ancient face, like the grim reaper I've seen in stories—gaunt, hollow cheeks; wide, empty eye sockets. He wears a flowing white robe. Flapping gently around him at shoulder height are his familiars: a clutch of iridescent bats. We see all this as he cranes his neck, tilting his chin this way and that in the direction of the houses, as if sensing his next victim with his ears alone.

"He's listening for the sound of people breathing," Aria says ever so lightly, so that barely even I can hear her. But even that whisper, from fifty yards up the hill, seems to reach the Griever's ears. He jerks his head in our direction and stands still for a moment. We hold our breath, and wait.

Finally he turns back to the house he is next to. He scampers through its dark window with the speed of a spider. Whoever the person is sleeping inside, I fear for them. I look at Germ and Aria, and we nod to each other, then walk softly toward town through the tall grass, watching for any sign of the Griever emerging from the house.

When we see his head appear at the window, we freeze, and watch as he scampers out. He peers back inside for a moment, watches, and bites his fingers as his bats enter the room. There is a dazed smile on his face. And then he turns and moves on, the bats following. He comes to the next house, listens for a moment, and scampers inside.

We move slowly down the hill, pausing whenever we see the witch emerge from indoors. We watch as another and another house is invaded. The bats flutter in and out of the windows, sparkling with what they have stolen. Meanwhile, we make our way closer and closer to the first house, and when we reach it, we peer inside.

Little One casts her glow on a man asleep in bed. A few bats are still here, moving over his body busily. A gray cat sits in a corner, staring at them and us, alarmed.

In his sleep the man stirs, and the bats flutter away and out the window. The sleeper sits up in bed as if shaking off a bad dream. He's maybe fifty years old, but he moves as if he's a *hundred* and fifty—slowly, as if it pains him. He stands and turns on a small bedside lamp, then walks to a table across the room where a photo sits, of a woman with bright eyes and long black hair. Staring at the photo, it's as if the man's soul has gone small inside.

The three of us look at each other, but don't dare to whisper a word. It's easy to guess that this woman is no longer alive. And the Griever, I realize, has made it so this man will never recover from losing her. By the look on the man's face, I can see that the unseen things that offer hope of what's *beyond*, and all the *maybes,* are far beyond his reach even in dreams. He gives off the feeling that deep inside, he is mired in a swamp. I've felt that swamp before, when I thought my mom would never love me. Maybe everyone has felt it. There is sadness . . . and then there is forgetting that happiness can even exist. The Griever's specialty, I see with utter certainty from looking at this cursed man, is the second of these.

"I've felt like that too," Aria whispers, looking at his face with pity. And I wonder what she means, and when. Who and what could have made someone as perfect as Aria feel like that?

The man crawls back into bed and holds the place where his wife must have slept. There is a painting of a waterfall on the wall beside his bed, and I stare at it, because for a moment in the dimness, the water looks like it's moving—though of course it can't be. And then a movement far off, seen out of the corner of my eye, makes me look up. I nudge the others. In being mesmerized by the scene before us, we've lost track of the Griever. He's skulking away from the village and up into the hills.

We reluctantly retreat from the window of the man so lost in his loss, and follow.

The witch is drifting farther and farther inland. We follow far enough behind to be out of earshot—at least, that's what we hope. And still the Griever keeps going, deeper and farther across the fields.

I look at my hourglass again. A red seventeen now spins inside the glass.

Where could he be headed? I want to whisper. But I don't dare risk the noise.

Finally, a little before midnight by my reckoning, the Griever begins to behave strangely, looking around like he is making sure he's not being followed, and then he slips into the dark gap between two large boulders. We follow, as stealthily as we can, though it feels like we could become trapped in such a place. We squeeze through the gap, and find ourselves in a kind of swamp, thick and hidden beyond the boulders and surrounded by impenetrable marsh.

It's a gloomy place, in the shadow of rocky overhangs where the bats now settle in. They hang themselves upside down, clinging to the undersides of the arching boulders, rustling like the skin of a dog when it shakes itself off. The Griever waves a hand at them. And—as with the chameleons—they exhale dark tufts of emptiness, as if changing light to emptiness inside their lungs.

The Griever gathers armfuls of these breaths, then waddles mournfully to a rock where he sits and pulls a spinning wheel, exactly like the first one we saw, out of his sleeve. As Hypocriffa did, he spins yarn out of the fibers, muttering to himself words we don't quite hear. Then, leaning back, exhausted, he hangs the finished ball of yarn from a branch at the swamp's edge, as if leaving it for someone to retrieve.

He lies down in the muck and goes, suddenly, to sleep. At least, I *think* it's sleep. His skeletal face remains blank, his empty eye sockets wide, white, and open. Tears stream out of them, but he remains still. And beside him, we see the container that surely must hold his heart, a faded trinket box that looks as if it could be made out of bone.

All around, the bats flutter and move restlessly, wide awake, as they probably will be till morning.

Germ looks at me meaningfully, points at the sky, and then makes a sleeping motion with her head tilted into her hands. She is suggesting we wait till the sun rises and the bats sleep, but I shake my head. That means waiting several hours we can't afford to lose. And by then, the Griever will be waking up.

I lift my flashlight, turn it on, ruminating. Little One, in bluebird form, looks up at me expectantly.

I think back to the story I told to Germ the day we met, about a bat that swallowed mosquitoes and burped out stars. The story came to me because, at the time, we had bats in our attic. My mom didn't even notice the noise, but I'd hear them leaving at night and returning just around dawn, when the sun was beginning to rise.

I close my eyes and think about those mornings: the calming of the bats at first light, the reassurance of the sun rising like a fresh start. A new day, I think, is the opposite of the Griever. It brings the unexpected, the possible things, the maybes. I can still picture it, the sun like an orange yolk on an early morning, bringing brightness after a long weary night.

I open my eyes, my flashlight pointed toward the ground. I imagine the sun rising despite the hour—a strange and impossible idea—but when I move the beam forward, a warm, round glow appears.

Germ lets out an audible, amazed sigh. Suddenly Little One resembles a ball that's caught fire. I look over at Germ, and we stare at each other in wonder. Little One has changed into a tiny *sun*, floating close above the ground, burning and glowing and golden bright. For a moment I can only gape at Little One—dazed by the beauty of her glow.

"You can make suns?" Aria breathes. She holds out her hands to the warmth of it as it burns brightly in the air.

"I didn't *think* that I could make suns," I say. I thought other animals was shocking enough.

I shift the direction of my flashlight's lens along the ground and into the air, a few feet away past the trees, where, if I were a bat, I might think a sun could be rising far in the distance. It's a trick of space and perspective, but miraculously, all along the rocky overhangs the bats' restless motion immediately begins to still—it happens instantly. Hundreds of bat eyes start to flutter shut. And finally, thinking its dawn, the bats settle down to sleep.

I blink at the light that's lulled them. *I have made a tiny sun in the middle of the night*, I think, again and again. If Little One can be a cricket and then a sun . . . what *can't* she be?

This time, getting the heart is easy. Aria takes it upon herself to tiptoe right in on silent feet, open the box lying in the mud beside the Griever, and slip whatever's inside into the sack in her hands.

Once she's back at my side, she slides her prize into my backpack. In minutes we are on our way, rising back into the hills and heading for the shore. As soon as I can take a moment, I look at my hourglass, still a bright and barely faded seventeen, and wild bubbles of happiness rise inside my chest. We will make it back long before our fifty-three-hour goal has passed. We are making up lost time!

We pass the town again on our way back toward the sea, this time poised before waking as the real dawn arrives.

As we crest the hill from which we first saw it, I turn to take another look. And catch my breath.

The Griever's footprints, stretched from house to house, crisscross the village below, outside every window and marking every road and pathway through town. It steals my joy for a moment.

I can see, looking from up high, how the footprints cover the town like a net. So many broken hearts, so much stolen light, and I know the witches have left behind towns like this everywhere, all over the world and all *over time.*

I remember what Homer the ghost said to me once, that chaos is to witches as water is to fish. How much of the planet have the witches entwined in this emptiness? How much goodness have they stolen? And what will become of the world if I can't defeat them?

I take one more look at the valley below, reminding myself that this is what's at stake if I let the world down. And we hurry on.

Chompy and Ebb are waiting to welcome us back when I blow my whistle, and soon we are diving to safety. Ebb and I almost try to hug each other, which is confusing, though Ebb's ghostiness stops us anyway. We've run down a little more than four full days on my hourglass. But we also have two witch hearts to our name, and I suspect Little One has powers beyond what I've ever dreamt.

We all lean over the kitchen table, dumping the heart into the snack bowl again.

This one is a flower—a red poppy wilting and going brown around the edges. Again, as real as the flower looks, when I poke it, the surface gives under my fingers like jelly.

"Every time I think things can't get weirder . . . ," Germ sighs. But she's smiling. We can't help staring at each other and breaking into grins, in fact. Because I know we're all thinking the same thing.

I'm good at this. That's the surprising thing. For the first time since we began, I actually think we have a chance. More than a chance.

I'm thinking we might just pull off this whole thing after all.

CHAPTER 14

It's terrifying and exhilarating and also completely weird, but we are a witch hunting crew, roaming the world, looking for hearts to steal.

Germ and I are in seventh grade. Right now, our friends are going to dances that Germ says are *awko taco* and learning to sew pillows in Life Skills class. Not *one* kid we know would even for a second believe that there's an invisible fabric surrounding them that includes witches trying to rule the earth . . . much less that I, Rosie Oaks, could be fighting those witches. I know that if we ever make it back to tell them, they won't believe us anyway. Mostly we just want our moms. We'd settle for any adult, really, who could help us. And yet here we are.

In the middle of a lightning storm in Russia in 1820, near a mine being plundered for ore, we find the Greedy Man—green-faced and asleep—nestled in a hollow of dirt underneath a forest of beech trees. He's surrounded by thousands of beetles—glowing with the generosity they've stolen from the owners of the mining company nearby—and sleeping in the space left behind by all the roots the insects have devoured.

Little One steals the witch's emerald-shaped heart by becoming a handful of caterpillars, burrowing into the leather pouch in which he keeps it, and slithering it out for Germ to reach down and grab. The whole thing—from tracking the Greedy Man through the rain, to getting his heart, to making it home to Chompy—only takes twelve hours, and we don't even break a sweat. A small clutch of hummingbirds passes us as we retreat, but our dimming works and they don't see us.

We find Miss Rage in the Sahyadri hills of India, from which—at night—she likes to shout at the top of her lungs (though no one living, besides people like us, can hear her) as she sends her sparkling hornets down into the valleys below to steal forgiveness and sow hatred in its place. I make Little One a starling that sends her hornets scattering simply by coming to roost in a tree above and giving them a hungry look.

That morning, hurrying back to our whale, a monsoon lets up long enough for us to see a rainbow arcing overhead. Afterward, it rains so hard again that we have to stop under a tree for shelter, knowing we are losing time. But with Miss Rage's heart in a sack in my hands, I feel buoyant with our success.

We find Babble living in Canada, near a small town where two groups are fighting over a statue in the town square, their words twisting like curveballs on the way to each other's ears. Babble's magpies, we deduce, have stolen their understanding of each other. The people are speaking the same language, but they don't really hear each other.

I make Little One a fox to scatter the magpies from where Babble sleeps in an abandoned school bus, and Little One captures Babble's heart, a tangled knot of thread, in her teeth. I can still hear the townspeople yelling from half a mile away.

At each stop, my hourglass reflects my time to save Wolf trickling away. But we are, shockingly, on schedule. We are even getting ahead of it.

✦ ✦ ✦

I don't sleep much. Here and there, we see the Time Witch's hummingbirds patrolling the shores, and there's always a chance they've seen us without letting on. Constantly there's the chance that the witches have found out, and that the next heart or the next stop is a trap. The more we steal, the more likely it is that they've noticed us stealing, that *someone* has noticed a heart missing.

It's like scaling the side of a cliff without any ropes. The closer we get to the top, the farther we are from the safety of the ground. I am so scared of falling, I lie awake at night in the glow filtering down from the Grand View, watching Germ and Aria sleep. I watch Ebb float through the cabin while he thinks I, too, am sleeping. He flickers in and out, letting his worry (for me? for us? for himself?) show when he thinks he's alone. I feel like saving him—saving *everyone*—is up to me. And still, I long for my mom, for a dad who is somewhere alive in the past, for someone to take care of me . . . and Wolf . . . and the world.

Meanwhile, at each stop, we watch the witches spinning, spinning yarn out of darkness, making a substance so empty-looking, it haunts me. We know it is Dread they are spinning it for, and it doesn't add up with anything we've learned about them. They're up to something beyond what our *Guide* can tell us or what our mothers and sisters knew. Whatever it is, the thing that unsettles me most is the *not knowing*. I wonder what the Time Witch is doing, where she is and where she thinks *we* are, if she even suspects we could be unraveling things beneath her feet.

There is one more thing that confuses me. There's the movement of the waterfall painting in Nigeria. In Russia, passing by a shop window, I saw motion inside a dollhouse, and I heard voices from a mouse hole in India. I wonder if maybe my imagination is unraveling my brain, if my imagination is truly running away with me at last.

I pass the long days on Chompy waiting for the next stop. I read my well-loved and well-worn books for comfort—the ones that appeared on my bed when we moved in. I study *The Witch Hunter's Guide* until I know it not just by heart but *in my cells*. (One thing I do not do is look at the hearts we've stolen once they're put away. I can't stand to do that; they are too gross, too frightening.)

I play with Little One, who's more daring and more wildly imagined all the time, a bird that once grew and shrank now able to transform into anything I can dream of.

"It's what *you* are," Germ says one night before bed, when I'm sitting on the edge of my bed flicking Little One into a shark, a worm, a butter knife, still troubled that it's not enough. "That's what makes what she can do possible. Your weird brain was supposed to be weird all along, Rosie. I always told you that." But it's hard for me to really believe it. When something has always been with you and made you feel different, it's hard to think of it as very spectacular at all.

And so the days go on, leaving me hopeful, and fearful, and worried, and exhausted.

And then we learn something new. It's about Aria.

We are in Iceland, 1683, tracking the witch named Egor. We realize it's him we're chasing when we see his peacocks strutting, unseen by the people around them, through the middle of downtown Reykjavík.

Unseen also, we've wandered into the heart of the city in the late afternoon, and there is a crowd gathered in the square, including a few nosy ghosts dressed like Vikings. A man at a podium is talking to the gatherers, the peacocks lurking behind him. We've arrived midspeech, but apparently he is mostly talking about himself. We guess this from the way he keeps puffing out his chest, pointing to himself, and smoothing his hair.

Whatever he's saying, we can tell it's boring. Beside me, Germ starts to drool because she's falling half-asleep, and Aria is looking at her fingernails. The man at the podium preens and swaggers and sucks in his stomach, and the crowd seems to love him. They clap and cheer every time he pumps his fists.

"I bet if we swam through the Sea of Always long enough," Aria comments dryly, "we'd run into ridiculous people beloved by crowds throughout time."

I nod, fearing, from the reaction of this crowd, that she might be right. It's with relief that we find the rest of the trail we are looking for—dark shadowed footprints across the white snow along the curb—and follow it toward the outskirts of the city.

We see it looming before us as we follow Egor's trail out of town. At first, it looks like a mountain amongst all the other mountains. But as we get closer, we see that it's oddly shaped, and after a while of walking, we see that it is actually *witch*-shaped. It's a mountain, but the snow-drifts that cover it have been carved, or blown, or piled into a sculpture: jagged chin, ski-slope nose, long robes, wide-open eyes. I'm familiar with this figure from my *Guide*. It's the shape of Egor himself.

"He must have created this as soon as he arrived," Aria says. "This guy's a legend in his own mind."

Does Egor go all over the world fashioning likenesses of himself out of any material he can? I wonder. It seems kind of pathetic.

As we get closer, the mountain arches above us, foreboding. At the base is a small hole that leads inside a snowy crevasse. And here is where we find Egor the witch, staring at us.

He's lying on his side facing us, his bed a sheet of ice. Around him is a circle of mirrors, also made of ice, that glint in the dim light of the snow cave like knives.

A moment of sheer terror passes before we realize he's not really staring at us at all, but at one of the mirrors beyond our shoulders to the left of the entrance. We stand stock-still for several minutes under Egor's gaze, but he doesn't move, or blink. In actuality, he does not look like the monolith he's carved to guard his cave at all. He is a small, gnarled man, withered and sad-faced.

By the bed is a tiny silver box, crusted with ice, where he must keep his heart. And next to it is the usual ball of yarn, dark emptiness spun into thread. Peacocks strut around him, ignoring us—they are too busy preening their feathers to notice us. We don't even have to hide from them; they're so preoccupied, they make terrible guards. They glimmer with what they've stolen: their victims' true worth.

"Is he asleep?" Germ finally whispers.

I shrug.

Aria, impatient, takes action. She uses her slingshot—not as a witch weapon but as its regular old self—to shoot a rock at the snow beside him so that if he flinches, we can make a fast escape. An icicle breaks and falls down right in front of him. A few iridescent peacocks flutter, but Egor doesn't flinch. "He's asleep," she says, and smirks. "He can't even keep his eyes off himself when he's unconscious."

Still, the ice box holding his heart is there in the mirror too, right where he's looking. He may not notice us, but he might notice anything interfering with his view of himself.

"What can you imagine, Rosie," Aria asks, "for a witch who's looking at exactly what you want to steal?"

Weirdly, I already have an idea. I turn on my flashlight, and Little One glows bright blue against the white snow. Then I close my eyes and imagine what Egor probably wants most.

I feel Germ shudder beside me and grab my arm. Aria lets out a small, strangled gasp. I open my eyes to see what I've created. By their fear, I know it has worked.

I've transformed Little One into Egor *himself,* standing there staring at us. But I've also made a few adjustments. *This* Egor holds a small Earth in the palm of his hand, as if it's nothing compared to the size of him. He looks full, whole, powerful—not hungry and empty inside. He looks like the real Egor probably wishes himself to be.

Now I shine Little One Egor onto the surface of the mirror that *real* Egor is staring at.

The witch shudders for a moment, as if surprised—and I worry I've made a huge mistake. And then his shoulders relax, and his mouth twitches into a smile. He softens. For a moment, believing himself to be bigger and more important than anything and anyone else in existence, he rests. And his eyes flutter shut.

As he does, I let Little One slowly, ever so slowly, float over to the ice-sheet bed. He bends over, removes the heart gently from its box. And then he drifts over to us and lays the heart at my feet before turning back into my brave, curious Little One, tilting her head to watch me. The peacocks, still too busy preening to notice us, never see us leave.

There's a ledge that looks out at the mountain range around us. We noticed on the way in that it looks down on a village nearby, and we sit on this ledge for a moment to catch our breath before our trek back to Chompy.

We stare out at the valley, just going dim, Egor's footprints crisscrossing the town below.

It's been like this again and again in every witch-cursed place—the trail left behind as the witches take what is hard in the world and make it harder, turning losses into voids, mistakes into battles, words into weapons. And the more I see it, the more I see that in every single case, their curses do this by separating one human being from another. And by separating every person from the trees and animals and the earth around them. As if all living things weren't a family. As if, in Egor's case, feeling more important than everything around you were really all that great.

It is while I'm thinking this that I see the woman wandering through the village below.

She is waddling down the main street of the small town, handing something out. She is poor—I can tell by the threadbare clothes that wrap her up against the cold—but she is giving out homemade bread to the people on the street. In the footsteps she leaves in the snow, a faint silver light glows and rises.

"What is that?" Aria asks, squinting at the woman.

I don't really know. The woman clearly isn't someone with the sight, and yet her footprints have that glow. But I finally share what I saw with the old man in Salem. I tell Germ and Aria about the man who saved the innocent *non*-witch Martha Parker. How he left light behind him, and how I read later that he'd saved her.

We stare at the woman as she disappears around a corner of a house, the silver light in her footsteps fading.

"Maybe it's not only witch hunting that pushes back against witch darkness," Aria says.

We sit in silence, thinking. We don't know what to make of it. We watch the peaceful village, children playing, sitting together talking and laughing around fires.

"*We* used to do that," Aria says thoughtfully, "in my childhood town. Before we left to hide. Sit around a bonfire together with our neighbors. It was like warming up the winter." She sighs, her cool teenage exterior gone. Germ and I are both silent. Waiting for Aria to share things about herself is like trying not to startle a butterfly.

"When we got to our island, Clara stopped making fires outside. She stopped doing anything fun or happy like that. She spent all her time staring into that snow globe. All because of what that store clerk had said, that a hunter had owned it. She wanted to believe there were other hunters in the world so badly, she felt like everything depended on it. I think"—Aria's voice catches here—"she was probably thinking of leaving for a long time, to look for them."

Aria hesitates, and doesn't meet our eyes.

"I started sleeping in front of the door. I was so scared she'd leave without me." She swallows. "But it didn't do any good. One night she . . . vanished anyway. I guess she probably crawled through a window to avoid me. It was like she couldn't wait to go. She didn't even say goodbye, or leave me any advice on how to survive without her. I don't know how she made it off the island. She was just . . . gone."

Beside me, Germ lets out a small sniff. I don't have to look at her to know she is crying. I am as still as it is possible to be, afraid Aria will stop talking.

"I guess she didn't want me to slow her down or be a burden she had to worry about." Aria shakes her head. "My snow globe is all I have left of her, really. I figure if she ever found those rumored witch hunters, they're all dead or worse. Either that or she didn't *care* enough to come back. I don't know which scares me more. All I know is that I'm so mad at her, and my voice—the *magic* in it—

hasn't worked right since I woke up that morning after she left, and it probably never will."

She looks over at me. "I know you keep trying to do things like I would do them, Rosie." At this, I blush, because I hadn't thought Aria noticed me trying to be exactly like her, and it's embarrassing. "But I'm just mad and hurt. That's all. It's not a strength, trust me."

Germ reaches for Aria's arm and links hers under Aria's elbow. Aria wipes at her own eyes, and then Germ's.

"I'm not crying, *you're* crying," Aria says, and smiles weakly.

We sit silently, my hourglass forgotten. And I take it in sadly, how Aria's grief and anger has broken her voice. I wish I could fix it for her, like I wish I could fix the things in myself I think aren't quite right, like I wish I could fix the world for Wolf.

"That's why I need the voucher," she finally says. "I want to go back to a day long before Clara left, when I wasn't so angry, and when I still trusted her not to leave me behind. I want to stay there forever. Even if I know it's not the truth."

I don't know how vouchers work. I don't know if *this* Aria would trade places with her old self, or if she'd just be an unseen presence, an unseen time traveler, lingering in happier times merely to be near them. But I do understand why Aria wants to go back.

She looks up through her tears, down at the peaceful village. The woman has appeared again. Her arms are empty of all the bread she was giving away, and she's waddling her way home through the snow. We've just left behind a witch who thinks only of himself, but the world is so full of people like this woman: generous, selfless, kind.

And then Aria does the thing—I guess—that helps her like stories help me. She hums, and as she does, the notes move like colors into the air in front of her mouth—the way warm breath puffs out on a cold day. She reaches out and touches the colors, poking them. They glow in the dusk.

Aria strings a few puffs of color together with her hands—a trick I have never imagined, much less seen. She raises her slingshot, tugs back the rubber band, and lets it flick gently against the colored puffs, which float down the slope and away from us, and finally over the woman walking through the village, like a lantern to light her way home. For a moment, Aria's powers aren't broken at all. But as quickly as her song illuminates the woman's path, the thread of colors floats right past her and into a snowbank, disintegrating, and causing a tiny cascade of snow to tumble to the ground. The woman's path goes dark again.

"See? Even when I try to do the most delicate things . . . ," Aria says sadly.

Germ tries to change the subject. "I'd love to hang out with those people for a night," she says, looking in the direction Aria's voice has gone.

"I'd love to hang out with *any* people," Aria says. "I mean, but I'm happy I have you guys."

Germ and I try not to react. But we exchange a look, both surprised by the compliment.

"You know what I miss?" Germ says. "The carnizaar."

I smile slightly. Germ's mom used to take us. It was a school fundraiser that was half carnival, half bazaar, with handmade crafts to buy. It used to be the highlight of our summer when we were kids. "Do you think my mom will take my brothers without me?"

"I can't imagine your family's doing anything but worrying about you, Germ," I say.

From our perch, we watch the rounded valley beneath us. The more I see of the world through time, the more Earth seems to me like a living creature—nurturing us, growing us, rooting for us, an intelligent animal growing other animals on its back, rumbling and churning and creating.

I try to imagine, for a glimmer of a moment, what it could be like if everyone could see the magic that ties them to the world, the moon, the clouds, the trees, each other—the beautiful magic that the black night reveals. Gravity was always there, invisible, and then we found it. Couldn't it be the same with magic, too?

My imagination falls short when I try to picture what that could look like. And maybe that makes me less of a witch hunter than I need to be.

But, in any case, the world I see from the ledge tonight is the opposite of witches like Egor. And it is worth fighting for, whether there is anyone out there to help us or not.

CHAPTER 15

It's evening, though day or night never matters much on Chompy. By Germ's count, it's our 105th day at sea. We haven't heard a whale call in more than a week.

There are bags under Germ's eyes, and Aria's jaw is permanently clenched. Ebb floats and flickers along the corners of the rooms, steering clear of me as usual, looking gloomy. I can see it on everyone's faces and in the way their shoulders slump. We are tired—more tired than any of us has ever been. The days and nights hunting hearts have worn us down.

Then again, we have six hearts . . . and eight and a half days left in my hourglass to capture the last three. The exhaustion of our crew is so intense, you can practically touch it, but we are also happy. We are, in fact, in very good shape.

Still, as miraculous as Little One's transformations have been, I feel like somehow I am falling short with her, like whatever I've turned her into is still no match for the Time Witch and what faces us in San Francisco. Occasionally I catch her giving me a look that seems almost bemused, as if my own imaginary bird thinks I can do better.

Germ—who's been playing solitaire for hours—stands up. "I need a break," she says.

"All we do on this whale is take breaks," Aria says. "It's a timeless whale."

Germ shakes her head. "I don't mean sitting around being bored. I mean a *real break*. Something different, something fun." She drops her shoulders listlessly. And then she seems to have a thought. "We need a party."

Reflexively I let out a groan.

Germ and I went to a few parties in fifth grade. (In sixth grade I was mostly occupied with ghosts and my mother's curse.) Back then, Germ always had fun at the parties, and I always felt like I'd rather be pulling my fingernails out one by one. One boy, who'd learned in Life Skills class that it was good to make small talk, asked me awkwardly which season was my favorite, and I literally ran into a closet. It was humiliating. But now Germ's eyes are widening in a growing excitement that makes me very wary.

"We need to have a seventh-grade dance," she says with finality, clenching both her hands together in fists.

"A *what*?" Aria says. Something tells me Aria's seventh grade was very different from ours, considering the darkness of the future. Ebb, who's been brooding in his room, lifts his head.

"A seventh-grade dance," Germ says. "It's great. There's soda, and music, and everyone's nervous, and you have to ask someone to dance, and it is a total disaster if they say no." Standing behind Germ, I shake my head at Aria in warning. Ebb all but disappears, floating through a curtain and out of the room.

"That does sound . . . great?" Aria says flatly, casting me a side-eye.

But Germ has latched on to the idea so fast, she's

unstoppable, a seventh-grade-dance juggernaut. "Chompy knows everything we want to hear—it's basically like he was born to DJ. And we should have a theme. Maybe oldies. Like, stuff from the year 2000."

To my surprise, Aria is beginning to look slightly interested. Germ has her at the music stuff. When Aria sees me still shaking my head, she shrugs. "Well, it's not like we're not in a timeless vortex," she says.

In the end, I am overruled by Chompy. I don't know if it's because he's grown partial to Germ or if he *was* actually born to DJ, but before we can even discuss the possibility further, the seventh-grade dance appears. Sparkling garlands materialize along the ceiling, and the Grand View monitor comes to life with a light show that sends colored spirals around the room. An upbeat song comes on. There are cakes and games and amazing party costumes hanging from racks that have appeared along the walls. There's a bathtub full of jelly beans, a trampoline, a Velcro wall and Velcro suits on hangers along a rail.

I decide, begrudgingly, that if this is going to happen, I at least need to dress more presentably. I disappear into the bedroom and try, of course, to do my hair like Aria, and put on some deep fuchsia lipstick and pull on a denim dress. I can't decide if I look nice or if I just look like someone sadly trying to look like a teenager and failing.

When it comes to fun, Germ is all business. She sets her chin and drags Aria into the middle of the living room floor before the last garland appears.

"Oh, we're doing this now?" Aria says, casting me a helpless look. Germ starts to twirl her like a tetherball, then grabs my hand and pulls me into the circle. And despite myself, I am soon doing some involuntary dancing.

I have to admit, it does feel a little bit good. Like letting gunky air out of an exhaust pipe. Eventually Ebb appears, drifting along the edges of the room skittishly, watching for the slightest motion from Germ to include him, so he can hurry out through one of the walls.

But, it turns out, a seventh-grade dance is fun. Maybe that's because only my best and most trusted friends are at this one, and in real life it would be different. But it does lift my spirits. Germ is right. A little dancing, it seems, goes a surprisingly long way.

For the rest of the evening Aria, Germ, and I find out new funny things about each other, like that Aria's favorite show is actually *The Wiggles*, and how Germ has never admitted—even to me—that she wants to be a pilot in the Alaskan wilderness someday.

Aria shows Germ how to do a French manicure, and Germ shows Aria how to stuff as many marshmallows as possible into your mouth while still being able to say the words "fuzzy bunny." Germ gives Aria the full lowdown on D'quan Daniels' perfect eyelashes, and Aria tries her best to look riveted. In other words, for a few hours, we act like we are twelve (and in Aria's case, fifteen). Only *Ebb* acts older, steering clear of us like a grumpy old man, probably because of *me*—and also, I guess, because he is, technically, a thousand years old.

But as Aria and Germ curl up in sleeping bags so that Germ can show Aria *Notting Hill,* a romance movie she has made me watch a million times even though her mom says we're not allowed because it's PG-13 and inappropriate, my thoughts of the witches and their mysterious yarn creep back in. So I slide out of my sleeping bag and climb to the Grand View and sit down. I open the *Guide* and look over the three witches we have left besides the Time Witch: Dread, Mable the Mad, and Convenia. Up beside the monitor, my mom and dad look down at me from the photo taped to the wall. I shine Little One on the floor and watch her pecking around—she looks frazzled, uncertain, weary, like the rest of us.

Then I feel a presence over my shoulder, and look up to see Ebb, hovering there.

"It's weird. Convenia," he says, pointing to the page I have open, the witch with the tired eyes and the cats surrounding her. "She's one of the weaker ones. She should have been one of the easiest to find. But now she's one of the last."

We study the drawing. She seems fairly insignificant, as witches go.

"You look awful," he says.

I glance up at him. "You're the one fading into oblivion," I say.

Ebb flickers with a smile. "What's troubling you?" he asks.

I stare down at the book. What's *not* troubling me? Still three witches to go, plus the Time Witch. Wolf still out there alone and afraid, in so much danger, not knowing I'm trying to save him or even that I love him. And then there's the strange spinning of the yarn. I know I am missing something important, but I don't know what.

"It's just . . ." I falter. "I've figured out all these ways I can use Little One, but she's still only Little One and I'm still only . . . *me*."

"What's wrong with *you*?" he asks with the hint of an encouraging smile. I shrug.

"I'm . . . messy," I say. "Like, messy in every way."

"Well," Ebb says after thinking a few moments. "What makes you strange and messy makes you strong. It's your weird and wild parts that are going to save us."

"That's what Germ said," I reply, "but it's hard to believe it. And anyway, I couldn't save *you*." I glance at my feet, a lump welling up in my throat.

Ebb looks away awkwardly. "What do you mean?"

I swallow. "I understand why you're not my friend anymore. I let you get caught by the Time Witch." Tears well in my eyes. "But I'm really sorry, Ebb. More sorry than I can ever say."

Ebb goes very dim. He looks, from what I can tell, surprised. And then he clears his throat.

"I didn't know you thought that," he says. He's quiet for a long time. "You know, I was in the Time Witch's basement for a few hundred years after she got me. I assumed she'd cursed you, destroyed you. During that time, I didn't even try to think about how to escape. I lost my will to try." He clears his throat. "And then I found out you were okay. That's when things changed for me. I decided to win the Time Witch's trust. I worked, I spread rumors, I lied, I stole. I spent a thousand years building up my crew and my reputation."

"You did what you did to survive," I say, thinking he's asking for reassurance. "I understand."

He blushes, and his glow brightens for a moment before dimming again.

"Rosie, I became the pirate king so that when the time came—when you finally came into the past and the Time Witch had you in her sights—I could be in the right time and the right place to help you."

I listen, my face flaming up. I can barely speak because of my confusion.

"But . . . you don't even like me anymore," I sputter. "You're not even my friend."

He looks away, and now it's his turn to look embarrassed. "That's not why I don't talk to you anymore." He seems to be searching for words that are hard to find. "It's just—after a thousand years, I'm not growing. I'm the same age. But you're already so different after only a year. I mean, you look different and do your hair different and dress different sometimes. You're leading a quest against the witches. You're . . . different than I remember. You've always been like my little sister." He frowns. "But soon you'll be older than me. You'll grow up and you'll live a whole life I'm not even old enough to understand. Like, I'll never go to a dance like you and Germ, you know? You'll do all that a ton."

"I hope not," I say. He flickers, smirking. "Germ's older, but you're still friends with *her*."

He shrugs. "It's not the same. Ever since you were born, my afterlife has been about *watching over you*. But now you're a ship that's gonna sail right past me. You're gonna outgrow me. And I feel like I have to start letting go."

This makes me feel embarrassed but also relieved inside. And I think maybe, in some small way, I understand what it's like to be scared of someone you care about. I've missed twelve years of Wolf's life, and it scares me. What will he think of me, if I *am* able to rescue him? Will he even like me?

I don't know whether Chompy does it on purpose or not, but a slow song comes on.

"Would you want to have a dance with *me*?" I say.

Ebb looks startled. I don't like him the way Germ likes D'quan; that would be weird. But I do feel warm inside that Ebb really loves me after all . . . enough to spend a thousand years trying to help me. Germ is still my favorite person on earth, with Aria running a close second. But Ebb is mixed in there somewhere too, in some weird space I can't define.

I stand and we try to touch our hands together. Of course, they don't really touch, but we do the best we can.

We walk to the living room and move around the room in an awkward but fun, slow way. We laugh at each other. We are like two people almost the same age.

Slow dancing is all the things Germ has promised: embarrassing and kind of nice. The fact that Ebb is a ghost, and a fading, flimsy one at that, doesn't make any of that less. I don't know where to put my eyes, so I look up at Fred in the corner, who's weaving the words:

I think that I shall never see
A poem lovely as a tree.

I wonder if maybe it is worth being weird and awkward and not fitting in most places if I'm the person Ebb wants to have his first dance with, and the person Germ sees as her best friend, and the person who can make tiny suns that put monsters to sleep, and do things that make my friends believe in me. Maybe Germ's right that you don't have to have a big group of friends as long as you have the *right* group of friends.

In the bedroom, Aria has fallen asleep. Germ is writing "fart" on her forehead. We are misfits. But also we are normal in our own weird, witch hunting, time-traveling way. Being misfits is, maybe, what everyone in the world has in common most of all.

And despite being hyped up on orange soda and Oreos, on this night, I sleep the sleep of the untroubled, and the loved.

CHAPTER 16

Germ and I are in our beds a few nights later, settling in to sleep, when I hear Aria's voice from the Grand View.

"You guys, come look at this."

We slide out of bed and walk up the front stairs to see.

The dates on our monitor keep disappearing, scrambling, speeding up, slowing down.

"It just started. I don't know what it's doing."

Suddenly we are rocked backward as Chompy takes an abrupt turn up. Stumbling back over my feet, I look at

Aria, who looks at me, eyes wide and afraid. It feels like Chompy is headed for the surface, but why?

"Where are you taking us, Chompy?" Germ asks, having fallen back against a wall, closing one eye so she can concentrate. But Chompy, instead of answering her in ESP, keeps swimming (no surprise there).

And then the numbers stop altogether. They blink and then go out.

It's too late for questions. Chompy slams to a halt.

I hear the familiar sounds that come whenever we emerge from water: the silence as Chompy's tail stops propelling us, the lapping of waves. Chompy's enormous mouth is beginning to open, and the dimness of evening is streaming in. Water pours in over our feet.

Wherever we're going, we've arrived.

The hot air that envelops us is steamy and moist. Ahead of us, we see a valley in dim dusk light, scattered with giant ferns at least a hundred feet high, stretching to the base of a steeply rising range of mountains, brown and rocky and towering above and casting evening shadows across the beach.

Chompy waits for us to disembark. We look at each other.

"Do we have a choice?" I ask, but I already know the

answer. There's a witch here; there must be. We have to swallow our fear, and follow.

We gather our things and slowly climb out, stepping into the warm seawater and wading onto land. I feel sweat collecting along my temples and running down the sides of my face. It must be almost a hundred degrees.

In the distance, the tip of a volcano peeks up far beyond the cliffs, rumbling and coughing. Every time it sputters, the ground beneath our feet rattles. The air smells thickly of decaying plants and rich, fragrant dirt. And the sounds of life are almost deafening—birds squawking, insects buzzing, and the growls of things we can't see and maybe *don't want* to see.

"That must be the problem with the monitor," Aria says. "I think we are back before humans kept track of time. Maybe before humans, period."

There's no question, this is not a place we could survive in for long. The volcano spews as if it will erupt any minute. We need to get out of here faster than even my hourglass demands.

"But why would a witch come here?" I ask. "If there's no one here to curse?"

I look at Aria, who shrugs. We are looking for the dark trail that will tell us where he or she has gone, when Aria holds an arm out in front of us and stills us. She nods up to the rocky mountain face ahead.

We don't have to look for the witch's trail after all.

We see him already.

His long gray robes dangle as he climbs the mountain ahead of us, scrabbling from ledge to ledge like a mountain goat. Unsure if he might see us if he looked down below him, we fling ourselves behind the nearest fern, and watch through the gaps in the greenery as he climbs. He keeps looking at the deepening dark sky as if he's hiding a secret from it. I recognize him, of course. *Dread.* The memory of the yarn and his connection to it disturbs me.

"Doesn't matter what he's here for," Aria says, as if reading my mind. "We only need his heart."

We follow at a distance, keeping to the sides of the jagged mountain. At first we climb easily, but soon we are scrabbling with our hands and fingernails, the ledges getting narrower and harder to find purchase on as we get higher and higher.

Germ, of course, climbs with her usual natural ability. She moves as if she could climb the mountain backward. Aria and I, on the other hand, are fairly certain this is the moment we will meet our deaths. About halfway up, Aria pushes her face against the cool rock and shakes her head.

I am feeling like my arms and legs have turned to jelly and that we'll never make it, when things begin to level off a bit. Soon we're on the top of a plateau, in a woodsy scrub.

We crest the rise and see the valley on the other side, waterfalls pounding down distant mountains, barely visible in the very last of the day's light. Far ahead, we see the bobbing head of the witch, still on the move. As we follow, staying far behind but always keeping him in our sights, night falls.

We walk for about an hour. As the night deepens, the magical things come out to glimmer: the Beyond sparkling and pink and far away, the strange and misty shapes of cloud shepherds crossing the sky. It reassures me that even here before "time," these things are present. But it's a fully dark moon night, and even the slim sliver we sometimes have to light our path is gone.

In the darkness, it becomes harder and scarier to traverse past bushes, over rocks, but at least Dread's trail glimmers up ahead in the dark. And then, at last, we come to a rocky outcropping where there is a kind of fissure through the rocks, and a clearing in the middle where he's come to a stop. We hide, tucking ourselves into the folds of the rocks from where we can watch the clearing without being seen. Dread has built a small fire and he's sitting near it, doing something with his hands. A rough-hewn sewing basket sits on the ground beside him, and I know without seeing what it contains: the yarn he's collected from all the witches. When I see what he's doing with it, I feel my stomach tighten with a warning.

He's knitting something. Silver knitting needles flash and glint in the firelight. Whatever creation he's making, it lies half-done across his lap like a kind of blanket.

Germ, Aria, and I look at each other, not exactly surprised that this is how the yarn is being used, and yet deeply worried. Dread knits and watches the path and waits. I feel a bottomless terror, watching him. It's as if he breathes fear into the atmosphere. It raises the hairs on my arms, makes the back of my neck tingle.

Something throbs lopsidedly in his pocket, and I nudge Aria. It might be his heart. Either that or he's got a bullfrog in there—breathing, moving, squirming.

But I can't steal a heart from this witch, I think. I can't even imagine going close to him.

And then what he is waiting for arrives.

Or rather, her hummingbirds arrive first.

"You're late," Dread says, as mildly as if a coworker has come late to a meeting.

From the edge of the darkness, the Time Witch drifts into view.

She walks up to the side of the fire, hummingbirds fluttering around her hands and shoulders. Aria clutches my arm, and we push back into the rocky crevice around us as if we could melt into it. We dim ourselves further, if that's possible. My heart begins to pound so loudly, I fear it can be heard from miles away.

The Time Witch settles on the other side of the fire.

"I was busy," she replies. Her reptilian eyes glint in the light of the flames.

"With your games, no doubt," Dread shoots back. "Gambling something. What is it this time? A piece of space-time from your sleeve? One of your little knick-knacks?"

"My games keep me from losing my mind, you know. Eternity is long and flat."

"Your games will ruin us someday. You take unnecessary risks. I hear you are taking them with witch hunters now."

"That's a bit dramatic, don't you think?" the Time Witch replies. "Besides"—she shrugs—"gambling against humans is like playing a game against a slug, or a puppy."

Dread is silent for a long time.

She sighs. "Have I ever lost? And besides, is that any way to speak to someone who's brought you good news across time?"

"Well?" He sits back. "And what is this good news? Why have you asked me to meet?"

"I've just been to the very edge of the future," the Time Witch says. "And conditions are ideal. We've spread enough curses around the earth to sever people almost completely from moonlight. The Beyond has grown dim for them; the moon—even when it shines—is distant. It's all perfectly prepared. It will be comfortable and easy for him, when he comes. A soft, warm welcome for a traveler who's journeyed far."

Germ and Aria and I glance at each other in confusion, wondering who she means, but for the moment, Dread looks as confused as we do.

"You've been making something for me," she says. She puts out her hands eagerly.

Dread holds it out to her. As he dangles it in the air, it looks like a half-finished blanket.

"It's beautiful," she says, deeply moved. Maybe there are some things new under the sun after all, for the Time Witch. This appears to be one of them.

"Will you finally tell me what it is we are making?" Dread asks.

"Isn't it obvious, by looking at it?" She holds up the dark fabric in her hands. It's missing a big piece, but still, its emptiness as she holds it up is staggering. "You really haven't guessed?"

"A shawl," Dread says blandly, annoyed. "An afghan. A table runner."

The Time Witch smiles then. I know that smile; there's only hatred in it. "A hole."

Dread is now surprised. He stares at her, waiting.

"Turns out the best way to reach a black hole . . . is with another one."

Dread stares at her another long moment, and then he, too, grins.

Aria understands what this means a minute before I do. She wraps her hand around my wrist and digs her fingernails into my skin. Just as the meaning is on the tip of my brain, Dread says it.

"We're making a black hole, to bring the Nothing King back?"

The Time Witch sifts the fabric through her hands, running her fingers along it as if admiring its softness. "It's really like burrowing a tunnel, from one place to another across the universe," she says. "Once it's finished, the Nothing King can step through it. And then he has only to grab hold of the world and drag it back in. Do you know what's inside a black hole?"

Dread shakes his head.

"Chaos. Obliteration. All of this"—she gestures upward—"the world and all the magic that surrounds it will be gone."

"And us?" Dread asks.

"We will finally have the disorder we crave. I can finally enjoy myself for once." Her teeth glint in the firelight. "I've been so very bored. Did I mention that?"

Dread looks both excited and terrified.

I remember Aria's words. *The Time Witch is nothing compared to the Nothing King. He's worse than all of them combined.*

The Time Witch shakes her shoulders, as if impatient. "Don't let me interrupt your other chores, here at the beginning of all things," she says. "You've come, after all, for an important job."

Dread nods once. He stands up, stretches his legs, as if getting ready for a day at work. He tugs at his gray robes, and something stalks out from underneath them. A hyena, glowing, hungry-eyed, starving, in fact.

"The first thief," he says with a hint of pride. "The first humans will be born soon, and the first familiars will be ready to steal from them. My pets will take their *sight*."

The Time Witch smiles at the hyena. "Who's a good boy?" she says, leaning forward to pet the creature, who looks as if he might eat her face if she's not careful. The Time Witch is unafraid. "Stealing such a gift from humans before they've barely begun. They won't see the Beyond, or the dead, or the goddess on the moon." She pats the hyena one more time, then stands, looking at Dread. "You will miss a few. They'll become psychics and have TV shows, and some will hunt witches."

"I know," he says.

"But in the end, it won't matter," she adds.

Dread tilts his head thoughtfully. "So the witch hunter you are toying with? She dies?"

The Time Witch shrugs, back to boredom. "Of course she dies. They *all* die—the twin brother, the loud friend, the girl with the broken voice, the boy ghost. They die in San Francisco, 1855."

Aria, Germ, and I look at each other. My stomach has fallen to my feet, and my mouth has gone hot and dry. And then Dread lowers his hands and opens his robes entirely. More hyenas emerge, one after another after another. They come slinking out—a slow, luminous parade—and spread in all directions along the top of the ridge.

In the end, hundreds of hyenas materialize from under Dread's robes, and lope off into the trees in the glowing darkness. They descend into the valley below to wait for the first humans, as Dread said. We watch in despair as they fan out over the surface of the roiling, young Earth, the seeds of disconnection and fear planted right at the very beginning of things.

People were supposed to see the magic all along, I realize with a deep, aching sadness—the light lying under the dark, the same living fabric shared by babies and mountains and birds.

"We should destroy them both right now!" Germ hisses. "Turn Little One into a beast that devours them both."

I reach into my pocket for my flashlight, but Aria stays my hand. "You can't fight both of them at once. We've got to stick to the plan. For Wolf's sake."

My hands shake as I try to weigh what she's saying against my overwhelming urge to destroy the witches before me.

Wolf. All this has been for Wolf. I can't abandon him.

And so, with the witches and their horrifying blanket in my sights, I hide. And watch the seeds of dread fan out over the earth. The Time Witch watches Dread's iridescent familiars disappear beyond the trees, and then she turns and floats out of sight, carrying an almost-finished black hole in her arms.

There is only one small victory.

At the exact moment Dread brushes past the fissure where we hide, Aria does the quickest, most *un-seeable* seeable thing I've ever witnessed.

If I weren't looking straight at her, I wouldn't even notice it happening. She reaches out with one arm in a smooth, seamless motion, and slips Dread's heart right out of his pocket. She is shaking as she pulls her arm to her chest. We *all* are. But Ebb's pickpocketing lessons have paid off.

We wait for several moments, and then she opens her palm to show us.

Dread's heart is a sleeping dove, a beautiful thing. But in her hands it shifts and jiggles like jelly, like all the rest, and I know that it is rotten to the core. It is almost too heartbreaking to look at.

Still. He may be the witch at the heart of all the fear in the world. But his heart is in my backpack now.

CHAPTER 17

We have arrived at our last stop, though we don't know it. I wake to a beeping.

Bleary, I slide out of bed and walk to the monitor to see what it means.

I've slept fitfully, dreaming of the campfire at the beginning of the world and two witches discussing the end of it, the black hole in the hands of the Time Witch. My first thought—aside from wondering about the beeping—is, *We lose, we die, I don't save Wolf.*

As the sleep-fog of my brain clears, I slowly make

sense of the beeping and what I'm seeing on the monitor. We are closing in on London.

Chompy must have heard the whale call sometime while we slumbered.

"It can't be true," Aria says, shuffling up beside me, rubbing her eyes and continuing a conversation that ended when we fell asleep the night before.

We spent much of last night—once we'd returned to Chompy and shared with Ebb everything we'd seen and heard—debating what we should do, whether we should give up on our plan entirely, or whether we should forge ahead. We decided, before passing out from exhaustion deep in the night, to at least get the last two hearts before facing the Time Witch, and then decide.

And now, suddenly, here we are. We're here to find either Convenia or Mable the Mad. There's no way to know which yet.

We still have plenty of time to get them both if we do everything right. But it's what comes after that we dread most: San Francisco, 1855. Where, supposedly, we die.

Germ, just out of bed too, is staring out the moonroof, her face drawn and pale.

"Why would she say it if it weren't true?" she asks heavily. "Why would she lie to another witch?"

Aria visibly struggles to answer this. "She was only talking about one possible future, one where we fail," she presses. "There have got to be *lots* of possible futures. The time-traveling whales make that possible. The future she's seen can't be the one where we've collected so many hearts."

Germ and I are silent, unconvinced. I want to believe her. But I can't help thinking of what she said when she first boarded Chompy what seems like forever ago. The Time Witch knows our moves the moment we make them. She's a cat and we're the mice.

Ebb is standing at the monitor, watching the years and places tick by.

"You know, Rosie, the London where we're headed to is in 2001. Your dad was alive then, right? He probably used London as one of his ports." He looks back at me. "What if we run into him?"

I know Ebb is trying to think of one thing, anything, to bring brightness to our dark moods. But I also know that running into my dad would be like coming across a pearl lost in the ocean. It's not going to happen. And then, seeing how unimpressed I am, Ebb points out something else. "Also, it's the home of Harry Potter," he says, giving me a look that's meant to be encouraging.

I smile at him sadly. Ebb does know me, in some ways,

better than I know myself. I've longed to see Leadenhall Market and King's Cross Station and all the places that my favorite stories have changed for me from something real into something *more.* And I do feel a tiny sizzle of curiosity, in the pit of my stomach, despite the sense of doom that's descended on us all like a thunderstorm. When we finally whir to a stop in the port of London, I am even a little bit excited.

"I recognize that whale," Ebb says, staring at the Grand View's image of the killer whale we've come upon swimming near the wharf. "I saw it from my ship once, a couple hundred years ago. It belongs to Mable the Mad."

"Mable the Mad it is, then," Aria says, her face going still with determination. I know she is thinking the same thing I am. That all of this could be pointless, and maybe we've already lost. But we have to try.

Chompy's mouth begins to open.

"*Notting Hill* was filmed here," Germ says, apropos of nothing.

And despite the heaviness we all feel, and despite the witch and the whale, and despite the newfound realization that there are even worse things than a web of curses over the world, for the moment I'm just a girl who loves Harry Potter, standing on a whale, getting to see London at last.

We find ourselves stepping out of Chompy's mouth onto a fog-enshrouded wharf in the middle of the night. The smell of rotten fish hits us like a wall, and we see the London Eye, a great twinkling Ferris wheel, in the distance, closed and still for the night but still alight. Big Ben chimes somewhere we can't see, along with all the other far-off sounds of any modern city that goes all night. But here, at the wharf, all is deserted and dark.

"There," Aria says, pointing to a dark trail that leads up the docks past a row of buildings, taking a sharp right behind a wall. We follow it, winding around corners past a string of town houses, a small coffee and antiques shop called A Gathering of Lost Things, a pub with a lion on the front. Soon it all starts to blur together as we make our way into the snaking streets of London. It seems we cross half the city in our slow pursuit of Mable the Mad, and a few landmarks I've read about stand out: the London Zoo, the Millennium Bridge, all mostly deserted in the dark. Ghosts congregate on the steps of churches and old stone buildings. Finally, near dawn, the trail leads us to a small, crooked apartment building with a narrow staircase.

We can see that the witch has already been and gone. We find people in the hallways muttering to themselves, sitting and weeping with their doors open, speaking to nothing and no one. Mable's dark footsteps mark the floors leading to each door. Her curse, among all the witches' curses, is particularly cruel. She doesn't disconnect people from each other; she disconnects them from themselves. They don't know what's real and what's not. As we walk past one apartment, I see the tail end of one of her rabbits hopping out a third-story window and disappearing into the night.

At the very top of the stairs, the footprints turn back on each other. We've come to another home with its door open, where a little boy is peeping out from behind a chair. There are no footprints in here, no sign of the witch, but it catches my attention because the boy is looking straight at me. *He can see me.* He smiles. He must have hidden from her.

I peer around the room. The TV is on, and cartoons are playing quietly in the background.

"Where are your parents?" I ask him.

"At work," he says.

He's here all alone, I realize, hiding from a terrible thing. I know I have to leave and keep following the footprints, but something draws me to the boy. Back when my mom was under the Memory Thief's curse, I was all alone too.

"Are you real?" he asks. I swallow, then nod. "I see

things no one else can see," he says. "Sometimes I wish I didn't."

"I know what you mean," I say.

Being different, I know all too well, can make you feel alone. And feeling alone can make you feel dusty inside.

"I saw a witch." He shivers, fear crossing his face. He seems to reflect on this. "Some things are so scary, they make you want to crumple up," he says.

I feel an ache rising in my throat. "I'm trying to fix some of that," I whisper.

"We've gotta catch up to her." Aria, who's been standing behind me keeping a lookout, tugs my sleeve. "Let's go."

I turn to follow Aria out, but on second thought I turn back. I pull my *Snowy Day* book—the one I packed for good luck what seems like forever ago—out of my backpack's front pocket, and slip it into the boy's hands. I can't really explain why I do it, except that when I was little, the book kept reminding me that there is always wonder in the world.

"There are beautiful things too," I say. "And you are not alone."

I look up, and Aria is shaking her head at me, an angry expression on her face.

"It's only a book," I whisper. "It won't make any difference. Nobody will notice."

The boy takes the book, and opens to the first page. I don't know if he will read it or if it will mean to him what my books have meant to me. But it's the best I can do. Aria is pulling me forward, and we move on.

We find Mable the Mad three blocks away, where she's sleeping in an empty Tube tunnel that has long since fallen into disuse. To lure her rabbits away from her, I turn Little One into a carrot dangling at the end of a string. It works like a dream. We retrieve her heart tucked in her sleeve—a piece of rope frayed at the edges—and soon we are snaking our way out of the abandoned tunnel into the dim light that comes before the sun rises.

Stores are still closed, but a few people have begun milling about as London comes awake. Up ahead, the antiques store we passed on our way in, A Gathering of Lost Things, has opened its doors. I suppose because they sell coffee and want to catch the morning commuters.

I'm rounding the corner to pass it when something brings me up short. It's a man I glimpse who's just walked in. Through the glass of the storefront, I watch his profile as he crosses the room. He looks like he could be a sailor, head nestled into a weather-beaten coat, hair windblown and messy, not the usual kind of man you'd see in an antiques store. There's something deeply familiar about him.

"I need to do something alone for a second," I say to Aria and Germ. "Is that okay? I'll catch up with you at Chompy."

"You sure?" Germ asks. I nod. They both look reluctant, but also, Germ can read all my faces. She knows when I need to do something on my own, and she knows when I'm determined. "Okay, we'll see you there," she says. She takes Aria's elbow and they walk away.

After they've turned the corner, I walk closer and peer in through the shop window, my heart pounding everywhere it shouldn't—in my knees, my feet, my head. The man is standing at a counter at the back of the shop, holding out his hand for the antiques dealer to assess what he holds.

Now my heart skitters so fast, I think it will burn itself out.

It looks, from here, like what he holds might be a silver whistle. A whistle like my dad found, long ago.

I hurry inside.

Considering it's not even quite light out, the store is empty but for the man and the shopkeeper. There are cracked vases, old coins, mismatched ceramic tea sets.

There are all sorts of old clocks ticking away the hours, each set to a different time. I make my way through the dusty aisles, past shelves full of lamps and jewelry boxes, toward the back of the shop. But when I get close, I see that the man is not holding a whistle at all.

He's got a handful of silver spoons, and he's trying to get the best price for them. And then I see his face. And suddenly I want to evaporate, or spill onto the floor and right through the cracks. He is not my dad. Of course he's not my dad.

I guess, since what Ebb said, I've been watching for him even though I didn't know it. I've been wishing, hoping against hope.

I turn back to leave. But as I do, I notice that something has changed. At first I can't put my finger on what. And then I realize that it's *silence*. The clocks have all stopped ticking. I look over at the counter where the clerk stands. She is completely still, her eyes frozen on one spot. The man with the spoons stands as petrified as a statue. Hummingbirds flutter around him.

And then I feel a pair of eyes on me. I turn to see a darkly dressed figure watching me from the end of the aisle, pocket watches dangling from around her neck. I yank out my flashlight and turn it on.

The Time Witch moves quickly and easily. She waves a hand, and Little One freezes in midair—stopped in time. She comes walking toward me. She smiles.

"You left a trace," she says. And she waves her hand once more, levitating my *Snowy Day* book out of her robe. She cocks her head. "I heard the change when you gave it to the boy. Like threads of time gone wobbly."

She sends her hummingbirds all around Little One, who is easily and quickly pulled onto the ground, flickering in distress. As I dive forward to help her, the birds surround me. They peck at me little by little. I try to bat them away, but there are too many. At first I don't know what the feeling is. My feet ache. My legs feel as if they're being stretched. And then I realize, I'm growing, getting older.

I am losing time.

We don't die here, I think, frantic. *We die in San Francisco.* But it's only a desperate thought.

I'm starting to feel my bones creak when there is a sudden, screeching sound. Something hits the window, and around me windows shatter in a deafening crash. Antiques come flying from the shelves; the clocks all burst into pieces. A shard of glass hits the Time Witch right in the chest. She stumbles backward against a shelf, and it falls over on her. Behind me, a wall crumbles and falls.

And still the screeching continues. I'd know the sound anywhere. It's Aria's broken voice.

In another second, Aria and Germ are standing over me in the rubble, Aria with her slingshot aloft, and I grab Germ's offered hand. And then we're off, careening out of the shop and toward the wharfs where Chompy's open mouth is waiting.

It flashes across my mind that if we were trying to avoid tampering with history, that's all over now. I don't see until we are rounding the corner that it's not just the antiques shop that's been destroyed by Aria's scream but the whole block. The fronts of buildings have practically disintegrated, and people stand amidst the debris, looking around in shock. Their eyes glide right over us.

"I'm sorry!" Aria yells, as if she weren't saving my life.

And then I'm hit by another wave of hummingbirds—we all are.

Spun by the force of them, I tumble onto my back.

The Time Witch is closing the distance before me—moving down the block. She's lifting her arms—to freeze us? to throw more curses?—when Aria lifts her slingshot and lets out another scream as she lets fly a rock. We are all blown back by the sound of it, including the Time Witch, who is blasted to the ground. For a moment, all is still.

And then we hear a piercing creak. In the distance, we see the London Eye shake, and with a heart-stopping moan of metal and glass, it begins to topple.

Even the Time Witch, still on the ground, watches in disbelief as the Ferris wheel crashes down with thud after deafening thud. It's just long enough for me to lift up my flashlight again. I try to think how Little One can save us from time itself standing still. But I'm helpless, frantic, lost.

"There was a place that saved us," I whisper, in tears, trying to picture that place in my mind, a place away from everything that scares me. "We got out."

Little One, flailing, disappears. She snuffs out. She's gone.

But where she vanished, a door appears—open, empty, and uncertain. I know it on sight. It's the door I used to imagine as a kid that took me out of my classroom and into the clouds.

Aria screams and shoots her slingshot again, hard enough to knock the closest hummingbirds back to give us cover. We run, all three of us, through the door, dragging each other along.

And then everything disappears in a blinding flash of light. And the doorway swallows us whole.

CHAPTER 18

I wake with a start, shielding my face.

After a moment I lower my hands, blinking into bright light. I hear birds and some kind of rushing water nearby, maybe a river.

Slowly I sit up, looking around and trying to make sense of where I am—a bright, airy bedroom with yellow walls. There are two other beds in the room, where Aria and Germ are deeply asleep under piled mounds of white comforters. Silently I slide out of bed onto shaky legs. I don't know where we are, but it doesn't look like a place the Time Witch would keep someone prisoner. Still, I don't know for sure.

Near the foot of the bed is an easy chair, with a cross-stitched pillow propped cheerfully on its seat. It's one of those old-fashioned sorts of cross-stitches that certain kinds of grandmas make, with a threaded picture of a little pink-and-blue house. But the cross-stitched words are curious:

> *You are the cloud-builder; you are the grower of wings. You are the one whom Earth entrusts its stories to; you are the singer of songs.*
>
> *Reader, look behind you. You have left moonlight where you've walked, though you may not remember it.*

I squint at the pillow, trying to understand it. Then I feel another moment of panic. I clutch at my hourglass necklace and lift it to see.

"No, no, no," I whisper. *NO.*

There's almost no sand left. The floating red number is a faded one, mostly gone. There can't be more than two or three hours' worth of sand inside.

It can't be. I keep shaking my head as if I can make it

untrue. My time to save Wolf, all the time we had left . . . it has almost completely vanished.

I am so devastated, I forget to be quiet in case we are somewhere dangerous. I walk out into the hallway, shutting the door behind me. I startle as I see someone staring at me from across the hall, then realize I'm looking at a mirror.

It's an understandable mistake. My reflection is me, but not a *me* I know. I touch my face. It takes me a moment to realize why. I'm older! I can see it in the way the size of my head has caught up to my ears, how my chin is more pronounced. I'm taller, though not what anyone would call tall. My legs have grown thin and long like the legs of a deer.

"She's taken a year from you," I hear a voice say. "You're thirteen now."

I step gingerly down the hall, following the sound into a round room surrounded by tall, wide windows, their sills teeming and spilling with plants. On one far edge of the room a woman sits with her back to me, guiding a needle through a cross-stitch on her lap and tapping her foot to music I can't hear. More plants sit tucked on shelves, in corners, perched on top of books and tables. It's messy and wild and disorganized.

I am a swirl of feelings: agony about the time in my hourglass, shock about suddenly finding myself thirteen, confusion about the Time Witch and where we left her and where we are. But all I can do is clear my throat.

The woman turns. She's wearing a brown caftan, her long brown hair falling around her shoulders. She is curvy and dewy-faced. She holds up what she's stitching so I can see it—a kitten dangling from a tree branch, with the words "Hang in There!" stitched underneath in yellow.

She puts the project aside and nods to a comfy chair in a corner. "Why don't you have a seat? You look out of sorts. Would you like some tea?"

"Um." It's all I can manage to get out.

"I'll take that as a yes." She leaves the room for a moment.

The chair she's directed me to has another cross-stitched pillow on top:

Come away, O human child!
To the waters and the wild
With a faery, hand in hand,
For the world's more full of weeping
than you can understand.

There are others around the room, a mixture of silly sayings like *Me? Sarcastic? Never!* and more profound things like *Anything you lose comes round in another form.* I blink at them as I sit, waiting.

The woman returns with a mug of tea. She hands it to me and I take a sip. It tastes like lemons and cinnamon. It's soothing.

"It's the little things," she says, smiling.

"Where am I?" I ask.

The woman shrugs and looks out the window as if gauging the answer to my question.

"I suppose we're over Ohio about now," she says.

"Ohio?"

"Well." She nods toward the window. "Maybe closer to Indiana. Have a look."

I stand slowly and walk to the window. We are surrounded by thick, rolling hills of mist; it seems to stretch for miles around. Far to the east I see the shifting shape of a cloud shepherd blowing at the edges of this mist, his cheeks puffed out and his mouth pursed.

And then I look down over the edge of the windowsill. That, it turns out, is a mistake: my stomach drops to my feet. Through a pothole-shaped gap in the mist, I see we are miles above the earth. Suddenly I feel the terror of falling. I cling to the wall next to me, wanting something to hold on to.

"Are we . . . ?"

"On a cloud?" The woman nods. "Isn't that where you wanted to be?"

"Clouds don't hold houses up," I sputter. "They're vapor."

She nods, agreeing with me. "Nevertheless, here we are." The woman begins to tidy up her sewing materials, putting them into a basket. The thread she was using seems to shimmer and move in her hands.

"Who are you? Am I dreaming? Am I dead? Are you an angel?"

She points to a small sign over the doorway.

BRIGHTWEAVER: MENDER OF SPIRITS, SOULS, AND HEARTS. FREE ALTERATIONS! ALL ORGANIC!

"I've been called different things by different people over the years. Fairy, angel, muse . . . I can't be fussed either way. I'm here to help; that's all you need to worry about." She smiles. "It was a close one. But you found me just in time. It's nice, I so rarely have visitors. Most of what I do is mail order."

"How did I . . . come here?"

"By imagining your way to me, I suppose. It seems to be your strength, witch hunter."

"But the Time Witch. We've lost." It's all landing on

me at once. The realization that our plan has failed, that my time left is practically nonexistent. "She found me in London, after I interfered with time and gave someone a book. The witches are going to swallow the whole universe into a black hole." I breathe. "We heard them talking about it."

The Brightweaver looks startled for a moment. But she doesn't question me. "I see," she says, nodding. "Well, I can tell you're weary." She lifts the corners of her mouth in an encouraging smile, though I can see I've rattled her. "A tour will help. And we haven't got much time together." She sniffs the air. "It smells like rain. We'd better wake the others."

The Brightweaver gives Germ and Aria a quick meal. ("You look older," Germ says, squinting at me in confusion as we sit at a round, wooden kitchen table. And then, her shoulders slumping forward, she says, "We've lost, haven't we?") Then the Brightweaver explains to them where we are. She leads us all out the front door, and we find ourselves stepping onto a trail that winds across the misty hills of the cloud beneath us, into a peaceful glade growing out of a valley in the mist. The trees, too, are made of vapor. In the air around us, cloud shepherds blow and herd the fluffy shapes of it. Our feet sink slightly beneath us, like we're walking on marshmallows.

But if walking across a forest of clouds is strange and spectacular, it pales in comparison to what we see amongst the trees. A towering, cloudy castle rising up as far as the eye can see.

"What is that?" Aria breathes.

The Brightweaver tilts her head casually. "The museum." She leads us down the path. "The cloud shepherds maintain it. It's taken them infinite time to compile it. It contains records of all languages ever invented. All the human languages of course, but also dog, bear, jellyfish, crabgrass, the carnivorous and non-carnivorous plants, local colloquialisms of mosses—you name it. Also," the Brightweaver goes on—proudly, "all the maps ever made or imagined, including ones of imaginary worlds, maps of the minds of each person alive. Sheet music for every note ever sung. Every picture ever drawn, painted, or imagined. Every dream ever dreamt. Every word that ever left a person's mouth. Who knows what else is in there. I've never been to the top of it, though I've climbed and climbed. I don't know if there *is* a top, to be honest."

We walk past a ghost sitting on a bench outside the

castle, reading a book that the cover says is a translation of *Eastern Volcanic Rock* into Spanish.

"How . . . ?" Aria asks. "How is that possible?"

"Simple chemistry, I guess," she says. "All those words and ideas and dreams are lighter than air, so it all floats up. And gets stuck up here, snags on the vapor of the clouds."

"How can dreams leave a trace?" I say. This does not sound like chemistry to me. "They're not real." I think of some of the dreams I've had. The one where Jennifer Aniston came to my house for French toast. The one where I was driving Germ to get her parachute license and eating a shoe.

The Brightweaver eyes me sharply. "Everything leaves a trace." She clears her throat. "But none of that's your concern today. Your concern," she says, looking at us, "is moonlight, of course."

She leads us into a glade, close and thick and mysterious. The trees are splashed in colors, in so many shades that I've never even dreamt could exist. Shimmery paintings with edges that aren't quite solid dangle from the branches of trees. The very air looks like it's painted, the sky above the trees covered in polka dots, stripes, bright blotches like waves.

"The art that people dream up tends to get snagged

in the trees particularly," the Brightweaver says, moving along. "The cloud shepherds will collect it all for the museum."

Germ is gaping down through another gap in the clouds as we pass it. "Wow, is that Des Moines down there?" She backs up, and bumps into a tree of mist, which dissipates at her touch. "Sorry," she says, blushing.

"Oh, it's fine," the Brightweaver says. "There's only one thing and we're all it." Then she smiles and walks on. Germ and Aria and I look at each other. It's not a comforting feeling, to see the mist that holds us thirty thousand feet above the earth dissolving so easily.

"A witch hunter's heart has to be strong. And full. And bright," the Brightweaver says as she walks. "There's no room to be wishy-washy, especially for you three."

"Rosie and Aria are the witch hunters," Germ offers, but the Brightweaver only plunges on.

"And there's only one way I've got to mend a hunter's heart . . ."

The Brightweaver turns at a fork in the path. We come to a small stream. Up ahead we see a cave; haunting music drifts toward us from within.

But the music is not acting like music should. It's attached to something visible and bright, a long, fragile, blue thread, as if it has been turned into a color and a shape floating on the air toward us. The thread of music ruffles my hair gently, touches my cheek as if to console me. It draws a pair of wings behind Aria's back and ties them to her. Another thread—alongside the sound of a violin—curls into a ball at the ground outside the cave in exquisite indigos and teals and burgundies, as if to cry.

"A lot of the music ends up in the caves because of the good acoustics," the Brightweaver says. "It'll be gathered up too."

"My music used to do stuff like this, when it worked," Aria says, touching one of the wings now attached to her, a soft smile on her face. The wings loosen, and disappear.

"Yes," the Brightweaver says as she steps onto a bridge built purely out of the round, yellow sound of drums, crossing the stream in front of us. "Music sneaks like vapor under doors, shines lights, leads to places you never expected. And here, you can see it. Up here in the clouds, I suppose you get to see what you've always known was real all along." She sighs, as if she's surveying a really nice garden. "I love that about this place. And I love that about humans and their hearts. All the magical things they create, it really adds something."

What she's saying reminds me of the things I've made

with Little One: the rising sun, the hopping cricket, the doorway to a safe place. I think about the one cloud shepherd I've ever met, and something he told me about imagination. *"Imagining is a little like the opposite of witches, don't you think?" he said. "To stretch and grow beauty from nothing at all?"*

"I wanted you to see all of this before I do my mending," the Brightweaver says. "To show you there are more ways of fighting witches than you can dream of—in the trail left by your mom's arrows, in the songs you sing and the words you speak. Every person's got such gifts. Anyone can fight witches, because everyone leaves traces," she says simply. "If only they could see all this, I think they'd believe in that more."

I think of the woman we saw from the mountain in Iceland, handing out bread, something so simple and small. I think of the man in the crowd in Salem who helped Martha Parker escape. Was this what they were leaving behind? Can people leave moonlight behind them the same way witches leave darkness?

"You three are not alone," the Brightweaver says as I try to take this in. "As much as it may feel like you are. Ah." She turns, leaning over a rough-hewn mist fence, looking at something beyond it. "Here's my favorite."

We are looking out at a valley, enormous, gently sloped. Cloud shepherds—there must be a hundred of them—are crisscrossing the valley, gathering something up in their vaporous arms.

The thing they gather is sparkling and pink, a lot like the color of the Beyond at dusk. And as they gather it, it hugs around them softly. Some of the cloud shepherds giggle as they work. The sparkling pink mist dances around them, sweeps under their feet, and lifts them up like balloons as they gather it—delicately. It's hard to watch them without feeling calm and comforted. And no matter how much they gather, more keeps appearing.

"What is it?" Aria asks.

The Brightweaver shrugs. "Love."

She smiles, then turns to look at us. "Okay, if I'm gonna fix you all, I'd better get started." She looks down at the cloud beneath our feet, which has taken on a gray color while we've watched the shepherds gather.

"Rain's gonna start any minute now," she says. "We'll have to be quick."

"What happens when it rains?" I ask.

"You'll fall to earth," she says with a shrug.

I look down at the world so far below us, my stomach swimming like I'm at the top of a roller coaster.

"You'll be fine as long as you stick the landing," the Brightweaver says.

And before we can ask how one does that, she hurries on.

My fear and worry about how and what the Brightweaver is going to do to us is growing, as we come to a pond glowing silver and bright.

"Is that . . . ?" Aria asks.

"Moonlight? Yep. I gather it in buckets on bright nights, when it's really coming down from above, and keep it in the lake to use later. I dye my threads with it. It's the hope it carries that I'm after."

"*Rosie's* been to the moon," Germ offers proudly.

The Brightweaver's eyes widen; she's impressed. "What was it like?"

I don't know what to say.

"Like a dream. I guess. Kind of like being here."

"I feel *bad* for the Moon Goddess," the Brightweaver says. "It's gotta be a big responsibility, creating hope for the world and all that, but she's not the best communicator. You'd think if you were going to fill the universe with magic, you'd also tell everyone about your existence, you know? It feels like sending a sealed envelope but you forgot to put the letter in."

"Dread stole the sight," I say. "At the dawn of humankind. Without it, people *can't see* magic."

The Brightweaver nods. It's clear she already knows this. "Yes, but still. Surely she could have come up with something better."

I feel the weight of her words, and the weight of my own distance from the Moon Goddess. The Brightweaver is only saying what I've felt all along. "It's kind of like she doesn't care that much," I say.

"Oh, I doubt that, very much." She lifts a basket of threads from the ground and dips it into the pond, shaking it around a bit. "You'll be surprised how the hope she gives can help people help themselves." Then she starts sorting some tools out of a basket that look rather ominous, needles both sharp and shiny. "But yes, some communication every once in a while would be nice. I like to think I help to mend the gap a bit, when I mend a heart. Though I know I'm only two small hands working against a tide." Her face grows sad, worried. "I try to stitch as much hope as I can into the hearts in my care."

She sizes me up.

"Anyway, stick out your chest."

"Um . . ." I look at the tools in her hand. "I don't . . ."

"I'll go," Germ says, puffing her chest. I stare at her in

awe. But then I've always been in awe of Germ's ability to charge into anything with courage.

The Brightweaver gets very businesslike. She points to Germ. It's as if a light has been turned on in Germ's chest, like when you are baking cookies and you turn on the light in the oven. (Germ and I always leave the light on when we bake because we can't tear our eyes away from what we're about to eat.) But instead of seeing the things you'd expect to see inside a person's body—a heart, bones, blood—a luminous, tiny lion rises inside Germ's rib cage, as filmy and bright as the music making bridges and wings. Its ears are only a little torn, its paws matted around the claws.

"I thought my heart was just a lumpy blob of cells," Germ says, eyeing her chest, her chin pressing against her collarbone.

"That's your *other* heart. The material and less important one," the Brightweaver says, seeing the wonder on our faces. "Now, I just need my needle and thread." She pulls her little basket to her side, and guides the threads she's dyed through one of her needles. "If you will face me, Gemma Bartley, and poke your chest out a bit more so I can get at it. It won't hurt. You are mostly good, actually."

Germ does as she's asked. And the Brightweaver begins to stitch. She doesn't touch Germ; she merely moves the needle and thread through the air in front of her, leaving thin threads of light behind that reach inside Germ and wrap around the lion—mending a torn paw here, a scratched ear there.

"Every person," the Brightweaver says, "who hopes to hunt witches has to hunt them in their own way. There's no such thing as destiny." She looks Germ firmly in the eye. "You're no sidekick."

Germ blinks at her, confused. But before Germ can say more, the Brightweaver turns to Aria.

"You."

Aria, nervous, swivels toward her, and her chest lights up. Inside, the shape of a bright red cartoon heart appears, torn down the middle.

The Brightweaver frowns. "You, my dear . . . Oh, I'm so sorry. Yours is just . . . completely broken. What *happened* to you?"

Aria looks away, on the verge of an eye roll.

"Her sister left her," Germ says. "She's gone, like, forever. And Aria doesn't know where."

The Brightweaver nods, still all business but with the tiniest hint of a pitying frown, and begins to stitch the rip in the middle of Aria's heart, pulling it tenuously together with silver thread. "I'm sorry, my love. I hope you don't mind me saying it, but you never know when you might be underestimating people, even the ones who disappear. Maybe you don't want to hear that." She sighs. "Anyway, I'll try to sew you up the best I can. But you're going to have to forgive her, you know. It's never good to let hurt turn to anger. That destroys things, as you might have noticed."

She finishes quickly, clearly in a hurry as she keeps looking up and turning her head, listening to the thunder that has begun to rumble nearby. Finally she turns and stares right at the center of my rib cage. I look down at my own chest in wonder. What floats inside—when the light illuminates me—looks like a tiny, haunted mansion with all the shutters closed.

"Ugh, look at you," the Brightweaver exclaims. "All dusty old rooms and hidden closets and dark basements. It's like you feel like you have something to hide." She pats my arm before she begins to stitch, her threads pulling open windows, dusting cobwebs from the eaves of my heart-shaped house. "Who *cares* about those who'd make you feel that nothing about you is right? Who cares about any of that when you have *friends*?"

I feel myself blushing. She looks at Aria and Germ, who look worried for me, then back at me. "Don't worry, I've seen much worse. Some have hearts that turn to mold, or mud, or porcupines, or ice, or sharp teeth. I can handle this, believe me."

She looks me sharply in the eye, then Aria and Germ. "But I hope you realize, mending you with moonlight isn't snapping my fingers and having things be fixed. It's only helping you toward being who you are. And I certainly can't patch a black hole, or kill a witch, or save the world. You'll have to do the rest yourselves, you three. I'm sorry, I don't envy you, and I don't know if it's possible. But being *certain* that things are possible doesn't really enter into it. We all must do our part anyway.

"Now." She leans back as the light in my chest goes out. "I do mail-in orders," she says. "So if any of this doesn't work, send it back. You'll simply have to have your bird make a doorway to me, or do what other people do, I suppose . . . wish on a star or pray or hold a lucky penny and hope, or whatever. But you will need to have patience. I have this one order from a man in Versailles whose heart is a puffer fish with clogged gills; he wished on a star three months ago, and I have yet to get his heart back to him. I'm way behind."

Underneath us, thunder rumbles.

"Better get ready," the Brightweaver say. "It's going to pour."

We look at each other nervously. Panic rises in my chest. Not least of all because I don't want to hurtle from the clouds toward earth. But also because . . . I don't want to face what's waiting for us down there, whatever that is. I want to wait a little longer, to put off the end of everything and probably the end of us.

"But we're not ready to go back," I say, raising my voice above the thunder. "The witches said they know the future and they win. We haven't found Convenia, the last witch we need, and we won't even have time now. I don't think we even have time to find Wolf. And I didn't get to ask you, since you know so much about magic and the unseen layers of it, about these things that I've been seeing all over the world. A painting of a waterfall in which the water actually flows, things moving in Aria's snow globe, voices from a mouse hole . . ."

The Brightweaver, her hand moving to replace her needles in her basket, pauses. For a moment, I've intrigued her enough to stop her in her tracks.

After a second, though, she only offers—haltingly—a thought. She has to speak loudly as the storm whips up beneath us. "All I can tell you is that the rules of space and time are bendable. There's a phrase," she goes on. "'A tempest in a teacup.' People think they're being funny when they say that. But rumor has it, a tempest really could fit into a teacup."

"What's a tempest?" Germ bellows. The thunder is almost deafening now.

"What I mean is . . ." The Brightweaver shouts something to us, but we can't hear her.

"What?" I yell. She says it louder, but we can't hear her reply.

Thunder roars. The cloud opens.

And, along with a torrent of rain, we drop from the sky.

Chapter 19

A speckled whale swims underwater, its enormous tail sending jellyfish swirling in its wake. In the open air above, there is a storm.

From within the belly of the whale, Annabelle can hear the muffled sound of torrential rain on the water above, though all around them things remain peaceful and still. They are closing in on their destination. Annabelle knows this because the whale is slowing down, its tail swishing slower and quieter, the numbers on the screen creeping closer to 1855. Up ahead, watching the numbers tick by, Convenia has not spoken since they left the coast of Maine. She's watching for something, waiting; Annabelle does not know for what. Annabelle still doesn't know whether she's a prisoner or an ally, a captive or someone the witch wants to help.

And then, in the silence, Convenia turns to her. It's only fitting, given all that has led them both here, that her first words to Annabelle are the beginning of a story:

"As you may know," Convenia says, "I am a witch who steals forbearance. I take that in people which is steady and thoughtful and leave something much lazier in its place: carelessness, rashness, thoughtlessness. It's been fun, I can't deny that. The fights when two people share this curse at the same time are quite something to behold, like sparkling fireworks. But I have this scar."

Convenia lifts her sleeve and produces a small tin box from it, shoddily made. She opens the box to show Annabelle what's inside—an object shaped like a small, leather-bound book, open to show that its pages are blank. Convenia's heart. It's scarred across the middle with a bright pink tear.

"Did a witch hunter do that?" Annabelle asks, staring at the scar. After so long not speaking, her voice comes out creaky and afraid. Convenia stares at her with cold marble eyes, then shakes her head.

"I was caught out in the woods on a full moon night, after

a witch hunter gave chase. I suppose it was in the 1300s or so. I was in a wide-open meadow in medieval Armenia when the clouds passed and the moon emerged. It burned me; the pain was excruciating. I almost didn't make it back to my whale, and by the end I had to crawl, the moonlight had injured me so." She shivers. "When you're a witch, the thought of dying—there is nothing worse. You see, it's not as if what you love goes on without you, because you love nothing."

Annabelle considers her words. She wouldn't want to die, but if she knew Rosie and Wolf were okay, it wouldn't be the worst thing imaginable.

"A human was waiting for me at the end of the trail," Convenia goes on. "She was a girl, no more than nine. I don't know who she was, but she was no witch hunter. Still, she had the sight.

"She knew I was a monster the moment she saw me. She knew enough to be afraid of me. And with one shift of her foot onto my sleeve, she could have held me there, in the moonlight to burn. But that's not what she chose to do."

"What did she choose?" Annabelle asks quietly, after a stretched silence.

The witch looks up at her. "She had mercy on me." Convenia frowns. "The girl believed in it, as foolish as that is. She knew I could have cursed her in return. But she let me go anyway.

And that puzzled me. And because it puzzled me, it scarred me, right here." She nods again to her book-shaped heart, traces the pink mark with her finger. "And now I'm not whole. I'm not all of any one thing; I have this seed of something else, of wretched mercy. And because of that, I can't let your daughter die. I can't let the witches do what they plan."

Annabelle does not know whether or not to believe this. The witch is a liar, after all. All witches are. But she still asks, "What do they plan?"

"We have to find your daughter," Convenia says, not quite answering. "And save her."

"My weapon is broken," Annabelle answers. Liar or not, this witch has brought Annabelle all this way, thinking she has a power that she does not have.

Convenia nods. "That may change, once you have a chance to use it in the service of your children."

Annabelle holds her arrows in her hands, sifting through them thoughtfully. In twelve years she has not even shot one successfully. Not since Wolf was stolen.

"Wouldn't you rather have one broken chance than no chance at all?" Convenia asks. "When they are walking into a trap?"

Annabelle looks up at her sharply. "Rosie knows all about the Time Witch, everything I could teach her and tell her. She has enough imagination to anticipate a trap."

"It is not the trap she thinks," Convenia says.

A silence stretches between them. And then they see the dark shadows up ahead. Ten of them, still beneath the water's rainy surface, waiting. Enormous, dark shapes just under the surface of the sea.

Whales.

"They're here," Convenia says, a tremor in her voice betraying her first sign of fear. "They're all here."

I wake. I am in my familiar bed, inside the familiar walls of Chompy the whale.

I roll over and look at my things—my books, my backpack full of hearts lying by the bed. Have I dreamt it all? The Brightweaver, the library in the clouds, the stitching of my heart?

Ebb is hovering in a corner of the room, watching me. He looks relieved that I've opened my eyes. But in another moment, that's replaced by consternation.

"You're older again," he says.

"The Time Witch stole a year," I reply, my voice sounding heavy and groggy. It takes a moment to realize that I am now about the same age as Ebb.

"Any advice," I ask, trying to lighten the worry on his face, "for being thirteen?" I think about things he said while we danced. How I know, compared to Ebb, I won't be thirteen for long. How I am a ship sailing past him.

"Uh, don't die," he says with a smirk. "It's not as fun as it looks."

I glance over and see that Germ is sleeping, and Aria's curtain is closed, so she must be too.

"How did we get back in here? Have we been here long?"

Ebb shakes his head, his eyebrows scrunched in confusion. "We were waiting for you, me and Chompy, at the wharf. But when we heard the commotion and saw the London Eye topple, Chompy dove. I was screaming at him to go back up for you, when you suddenly appeared in your beds, all three of you. I couldn't believe it. I thought for sure you'd been lost forever."

I slide to sit up in the bed. Ebb moves as if to reach for my hand, but then—either because he's a ghost and can't *hold* a hand or because I'm older again, or both—he leans back. "You were talking in your sleep about haunted mansions. I couldn't wake you. What happened to you? How did you just appear here?"

I shake my head too, because even *I* can't explain it. But then Germ's voice chimes in from her bed.

"We went to the sky because Rosie made a door to

her happy place," she murmurs, slowly sitting up. "There was, like, an infinite museum. And this lady who was an angel or a fairy or something. And basically we learned that nature talks, like you always say, and it's all translated in books. I'm going to try to learn Iguana when I get home."

"*That's* what you got out of that whole thing?" I say, swiveling. "That you can learn Iguana?"

Germ shrugs as if to say, *Why wouldn't it be?*

We tell Ebb the rest, and Aria eventually shuffles out from behind her curtain in silk pajamas and fuzzy fuchsia slippers to fill in the bits we miss—the Brightweaver, the hole through which we could see Ohio, the power of unseen things, the mending of our hearts.

Ebb listens to it all as if, at this point, nothing would surprise him, as if he is very tired of magic in general. But also, very relieved we are okay.

I do feel a little different in my chest. It's like this tiny voice that's always been inside me, asking if a quirky, messy person like me is the *right* kind of person to be heroic and brave, that voice has gone quieter.

"Well," Ebb says, "we're already stopped. We've been swimming all night."

"Swimming where?"

He gives me a look but doesn't answer. My heart flutters at the warning and worry in his eyes.

And then I rise to take a few steps toward the Grand View and see the monitor. And fall silent.

"Ebb, we're in 1855."

Ebb flickers. And a fear grips me tight in my stomach. *We are here. We are here, we are here, we are here.*

In the swirling images, I see an enormous shadow in the water. It's another whale. Looking around, I see even more. We hear the whales calling softly to each other.

"Their whales are here." Which means . . .

"The witches are here," Aria says, her face drawn and shocked.

"But . . . the Time Witch found us in London. What if she knows?" I say. "If she knows we stole a heart from Mable the Mad, she knows we're stealing them from all of them."

"Even if she does, that doesn't change the main thing," Ebb says. "You still have the hearts."

He's right. I look at my backpack, slouched at the foot of my bed. I heft it into my hand, feeling the jiggly weight of the hearts inside.

"We won't have time to steal Convenia's," I say. "We only have a couple of hours, at most." I look around to see if all the witches' whales are accounted for, but in the shadows, with the movement of the whales, I can't be sure. I hold up my hourglass; the very faded red one is spinning in the bottom half. "It'll take all that just to find Wolf, and that's if we're lucky. When and if we fight the Time Witch, I guess we'll have to fight Convenia, too."

This seems beside the point now. There is ice in my lungs. But I know we have no choice.

Aria agrees.

"They'll probably be waiting to attack us as soon as we surface," she says.

"Well." Germ stomps her feet a little, like a bull spoiling for a fight. "We'll attack first. You've gotta have Little One ready to eat the hearts. Have your backpack ready."

Aria paces nervously, clearly feeling uncertain as she grips her slingshot, as if she could will it into working better. We look at each other; my breath rattles in my chest. We could stay here, safe and timeless, forever. That has never been more tempting than it is at this moment. How do you bet everything on something that is far from certain, even likely to fail?

"Are you sure you all want to do this?" I ask them. "Our plan?" I could go alone. I *should* go alone. But Germ and Aria don't even grace this with a response.

"I could come with you guys too," Ebb says. "Maybe I'd last long enough to help."

"Most likely," Aria replies, "you'd flicker out and disappear forever. Who knows how much time onshore would finish you."

Ebb nods. Clearly he knows she's right, but he hates it.

Chompy is swishing his tail, facing the shore, but he is waiting. All we have to do is rise, and we'll be in my brother's time and place. So close to where he lives and breathes . . . scared, alone, and never in a million years expecting me.

I can't help but imagine what we must look like from the outside, from an unseen eye—maybe the Moon Goddess's—looking into the sea: a whale, enormous but small in a vast ocean, surrounded by other whales and facing a shore where all the witches on the planet wait for us.

I think how once there were two babies born in a hospital in Maine. The first a loud baby, crying, a boy. The second a girl, and one who liked to keep to herself. I didn't always know it, but all this time, all my *life* really, I've been waiting to be here. To see my brother again. And to destroy the ones who took him, the ones who want to take everything.

It could go one way or the other. Only minutes from

now. We could lose. We *do* lose, according to the Time Witch.

Listening, I notice that the rain has stopped.

I nod. I clutch my flashlight to my chest, and turn it on. Little One hovers above me. Aria holds tight to her slingshot because it's the only thing she's got. Germ looks like she wishes she had a weapon, but she also looks determined to do whatever small things she can. I hoist my backpack full of hearts onto my back, comforted and terrified by the weight of it and what it holds: the key to our victory or loss, tucked into a JanSport Classic.

"Okay, Chompy. Take us up," I say.

We rise.

CHAPTER 20

The witches are not waiting for us on the shore. They don't attack us as Chompy rises out of the water to let us out. They don't even attack us when I see my brother for the first time.

It happens like this.

It's a cold wet evening, we find, as we breach the ocean's surface in 1855. Chompy opens his mouth, and fog pours in around our feet along with the ice-cold seawater. With our weapons poised, we wait for an attack, peering around into the mist that surrounds us, nearly blinded by it. It's the perfect moment for them to set upon us. But nothing comes.

We slide out of Chompy's mouth into the shallows, hearts pounding, sure that at any moment we'll see a flash of a hummingbird's wing, the glimmer of a hyena's eye, a witch's hand reaching to touch and curse us in the dimness of the early dark moon night. But nothing. We walk, waterlogged, onto the beach, soaked up to our knees and shivering. It isn't easy when everything's engulfed in fog, but we can just make out the dark shapes of hills and gullies in the distance. And one thing is clear. We are alone, for now.

I tug my hourglass and watch the sand trickle again. It's so little time, and already I feel like I am vibrating with stress. We have to move fast. I feel the kind of shiver that goes through you when you are near the end of a race. It's when you are closest that you feel the most like you can't go on, that the possibility of losing is too terrifying.

"I thought California was warm," Germ says, wrapping her arms around herself, shivering.

"The coldest winter I ever spent was a summer in San Francisco," Aria offers.

"You've been here before?" Germ asks, blinking at her.

Aria sighs. "It's Twain."

Germ shrugs. She's always been too restless to read, but I make a mental note of the quote.

The fog blows off for a few moments, revealing empty rolling land and a wide dusty road ahead of us. We see buildings far in the distance, their flickering lights (gas, I'm guessing; I don't think there's electricity *back now*) dim in the fog. The city of San Francisco. But there's no witch trail. No dark footprints leading us in the right direction. Nothing.

"They might've gathered up their tracks. Since they expect us here," Aria says.

"Well, what do we do if there are no tracks?" I ask, my stomach starting to burn with panic. Not that I expect Aria to have all the answers. I thought—I was *sure*—the witches would be wherever we turned up, ready to pounce on us. But I don't even see a single hummingbird patrolling the shore. It's extremely unextreme.

"We find Wolf anyway," Aria says, staying collected—though her eyes betray doubt. "That's what we do."

We're all acutely aware that we have only about two hours before the Time Witch snatches all the remaining years of my brother's life away from him. I try not to think of what that means. I turn to Germ, who's looking out at the water, staring very intently at Chompy.

She notices me watching her. "I'm telling him that when we get back, we might have witches on our tail," she says. "I'm telling him we're going to need all the help we can get." Her eyes dart to mine, embarrassed. "And I'm telling him I love him. I hate to be the one who says it first."

Aria and I look at each other. I turn Little One toward the ground to light our way.

We walk.

The harbor echoes with the sounds of bells and city voices carried by the fog. The mist comes and goes as we trudge on, sometimes obscuring what's in front of us and sometimes drifting to reveal ships beyond the shore, an observatory on a scrubby hill, busy boulevards up ahead, dirt roads leading out of town, orderly rows of buildings and houses. Ghosts drift around us as we pass through a gorge gouged out between two hills, for a few minutes losing sight of the sea.

"The gold boom," Aria says, low, as we enter the outskirts of the city. "I bet none of this was here a few years ago. We learned about it in school the year before Clara and I fled. Even then, all our history books were disappearing—stolen by people who were already cursed, to mess with things."

A noise startles us, and I cling tight to the straps of my backpack and hold my flashlight like a dagger. But it's only a slamming door. We hear an old-time piano playing somewhere. We pass buildings busy with people who are out and about for the evening. They all look past and through us. A street marked CLAY appears to be the main road, lined with stores: a shoe shop, a grocer, a hat shop, a drugstore, hotels, a dentist, all their lights flickering to welcome evening customers.

"Can you imagine going to the dentist in 1855?" Germ says, trying to buck up our sagging spirits, our agitation at the trickling time. "I'd rather let my teeth fall out."

We wander the city as quickly as we can, all the way to the other end. But nothing. No sign of witches, of Wolf, of anything.

This is not what I expected at all. And I realize, with feelings like ice spilling down my spine, *this is how they beat us*. We just go on wandering around and around San Francisco until our time is up. I see the same realization and fear mirrored back to me by Aria and Germ, the looks in their eyes, how Germ has started to wring her hands. Horrified, I check my hourglass with shaking fingers. The one has almost vanished—only the base of it remains, a tiny red line spinning in air. The sand is almost gone.

"This is how it ends?" I whisper, my throat aching. "This is how we lose him forever?"

We are standing there looking at each other, our eyes welling up all at the same time, when something grabs our attention.

Someone is whistling. And the thing that gets us is that the song could not possibly be from 1855. It sounds distinctly like someone is whistling "Don't Stop Believin'."

We turn to see a man standing in a doorway, watching us. For a moment, his tune wavers, and when he starts again, the song sounds more like "Jingle Bells." He's dressed in a vest and trousers, with a handlebar mustache and a long wooden cane in one hand. He looks nervous.

Finally he goes silent. He begins to walk toward us but doesn't look at us. As he reaches us, he crouches as if to tie his shoe and whispers, "You with the League of Witch Hunters?"

I blink at him. I don't have the heart to tell him we *are* the league of witch hunters. Witch *hunter*, if you don't count broken slingshots.

"I've seen her. The Time Witch," he says.

My mouth drops open, trying to form words. But he doesn't wait for us to speak before he continues, still kneeling in the road, making a double knot. "I know where she hides. Wherever the rest of your group is, you'll need all of them to get through her."

"The r-rest . . . ," I stammer quietly, glancing around the street to make sure we are not being watched, "are coming?"

I don't want to put a foot wrong and have this strange man give up on us altogether. For the moment, his hope is our only hope.

The man gives a slight nod. He stands, and turns, and makes his way back across the road. He pauses once and throws a look at us over his shoulder and leans on his cane for a minute before continuing down an alley that runs alongside the hotel.

"Should we follow?" I ask Aria and Germ. I lift my hourglass and look at the time, feeling sick. Half an hour left, more or less. "It could be a trap."

"I don't know if we have a choice," Aria says.

We cross the street and trail down the alley. Things get quieter and quieter as we walk several paces behind the mustached man. I pull my backpack off my shoulders and hold it tight to my chest, ready to whip the hearts out at any moment for Little One to eat.

The man does not acknowledge our presence again; if he hadn't spoken with us, I'd assume he didn't even know we were there. And then, so subtly that we almost miss it, he nods and lifts his cane, pointing it down a dark street.

Apparently this is where his courage gives way. Before we can get our bearings or understand where he's pointing, he's already gone, turning down an alleyway and vanishing from sight.

We are standing in front of a row of gas-lit brick buildings that look abandoned and very tucked away.

"He didn't tell us where," Aria says, pulling at her fingers in frustration. "Which building?"

Mere minutes left, and we're as confused as we were before the man *helped* us at all. But a moment later, I find myself staring at a doorway across from us. The hairs are standing up at the back of my neck. The wide double doors of the entrance look familiar to me, as if I've been here in a dream. And then I realize why.

"This is the place where Wolf had his photo taken," I breathe. "The one the Time Witch gave me. He was standing right here."

There's no mistaking it, I've memorized it so deeply: my brother's terrified expression, the intricate pattern of the paneling in the flicker of gaslight, the crack in the wood at the top of the right-hand door. He is *close*.

I walk up to the building and touch the bricks, run my

hands along them. I get on tiptoes to look in through a high, small window. Dim.

And then I see a hummingbird flutter down a hallway inside, glowing in the dimness.

"She's in there," I say. Which means Wolf must be too.

I try the door, absolutely certain it will be locked. But it swings open, quietly and easily.

"Rosie, it's too easy," Aria whispers, holding on to my sleeve. I know she's right. We are so close to running out of time, but also, this could still be a trap. But again, what choice do we have? Mentally I try to dim myself down to zero. My fingers tremble on the door.

We enter and find ourselves in a deep and obscure corner of a long hallway. We duck back into the alcove of the doorway a second before a smattering of hummingbirds flutters past, and hold our breath until they're gone, concentrating on staying dim.

As we step into the hall again, I see we have to choose a hallway to the left or to the right. I choose left, and we come to another intersection, where I choose right. Then left, then right again. The hallways are all the same—all musty and dim and empty. We are at another corner, and I'm beginning to lose my grip on staying calm, when a glowing ghost in a bowler hat floats by, wringing his hands and failing to notice us. He looks nervous. As we watch him get farther down the hall, casting a soft glow as he goes, I think maybe we should follow him. If he's scared, it might have something to do with the Time Witch. Maybe he's a prisoner like Ebb was. Maybe that's why he's so afraid.

I nod to the others, and we follow on soundless feet, staying dim with all our strength.

After a couple of minutes of winding up and down corridors, the ghost visibly stiffens. I see him shiver and shrink as he passes an archway at the end of the hall. It's as if whatever is beyond that archway is dangerous to him.

Once he's rounded the corner, we approach the opening. Aria clutches my wrist, ready to run. Pressing myself into the shadows of the wall to its right, I peer around the corner. It is hard to believe what I see.

I am looking across an inner courtyard that lies at the heart of the building, dim and dark and lit by gas lanterns, open to the moonless sky. In the far corner is a silhouette I'd know anywhere, a familiar black sleeve. The Time Witch is sitting in a wooden chair, turned away from us. She's got a blanket full of nothing on her lap—is knitting the last ragged, undone edges of it. To her left, an hourglass that matches mine—only much bigger—sits on a wooden stand beside her chair. The sand at the top is just about gone.

As clever as she is, it doesn't seem as though she knows we're here. A female ghost in old-fashioned riding clothes is equally ignorant of our presence, standing in the corner of the courtyard, waiting on the witch patiently and looking petrified.

"Shall I bring the boy?" the ghost finally asks. "It's almost time to take his years."

I swallow.

The witch keeps her face turned down to her knitting, slipping knots of emptiness over her needles as if deeply relaxed. It scares me that she isn't even keeping watch for us. Why isn't she nervous? Why isn't she trying to find us and fight us? Where are all the other witches?

"He has about ten minutes left. No need to rush," she replies. "I play fair."

Aria tugs my sleeve again. She gives me a look, and I know what she's thinking: we've got to find Wolf NOW. She's got to be keeping him close by.

Luckily, at that moment, the Time Witch turns even more fully away from us, picking something like lint off the top of her shoe. We slip away from the archway and hurry down the corridor ahead of us. With each footstep I wait for the Time Witch to burst into the hall behind us, to appear in front of us with her birds. But nothing comes. We round another corner, beginning to breathe again, and it's at that moment I hear something that makes my skin tingle.

The sound is familiar, but I can't place it at first. All I know is that it reminds me of *home*, in some way I can't describe. I follow the sound, winding left, then right, deeper into the building.

I end up at a nondescript wooden door, slowing to hear the sound still issuing from behind it. At the height of my knees there's a small metal slot—like the kind you might find in jail, where they slide meals to prisoners.

Chills cascade in waves down my skin. This is a place where someone is being kept.

Breathless, I kneel. Beside me, Germ and Aria kneel too.

The room contains a single shape of a person, standing and facing a wall. He is small, fragile and thin. A boy. I can't see his face, only the back of his head.

I start to feel dizzy, as if I'm floating above myself. Beside me, Germ sucks in her breath.

I take in several things at once. The sadness of the boy's posture, even from the back. The grimness of the room. The strange knickknacks along the ledges of the walls:

pebbles, old corks, pieces of broken glass. This prisoner has collected anything and everything he could get his hands on—no matter how useless or broken or small. Most of all, I notice what he's doing.

He is *painting*.

That is the sound of home I heard.

He has fashioned a brush and paint out of old frayed rope, a cup of water, and gathered ash heaped in a broken wooden bowl. I try to fight back the tears that flood my eyes. He is painting, like our mom.

Beside him sits a small tray with a candle that has almost run out, cobbled together out of old pieces of wax. He steps to the side to dip his brush in water, and when he does, he moves out of the way of the candlelight, and I gasp. The candle illuminates the walls of the room . . . and shows what a boy trapped for many years, with nothing to do, has accomplished.

Every inch of the cell is covered in paintings. Floor to ceiling, hundreds of pictures are sketched all over the walls. The lowest ones are rudimentary, as if he did them when he was very young. The higher ones are intricate, beautiful, haunting: a house on a hill, groups of people holding hands, someone yelling into the air, a ladder dangling from the moon seen through the bars of a window, a gathering of witches like crows. I know two things at once, from this room: Wolf has the sight. And he contains more darkness and light than I could ever imagine.

His drawings are half hope, half nightmare: tornados, beasts, rainbows, earthquakes, tidal waves, floods, angels, spinning beautiful planets. I can see in Germ's eyes what she's thinking. *What do you expect from a boy raised by witches?*

And then I see one painting in particular that makes my hands shake: two babies lying side by side, their little hands clasped tightly together. The second baby is dimmer than the first, and shaded. But it is me. I know it's me, because the babies are like two halves of each other, mirror images. Just like I always knew there was some piece of me missing, Wolf has clearly always known too.

I am almost too shocked to move.

I do not have to fight the witches.

I can free him, right now.

I feel a strange tickling at the back of my neck and along my back, but I ignore it.

"Rosie, I don't like this," Aria whispers. "Something is very, very wrong about this."

But I ignore *her*, too. I can't think of anything but the boy in the cell.

All my life, because of my mom's curse, I thought I

knew what loneliness was. But I always had Germ. And hope. And now I see what being alone really is, and that my brother knows it so much better than me. And, of all the things I've seen the witches bring, all over the world, I think it might be feeling alone that's the worst.

And then Wolf steps back to the wall with his freshly dipped brush, and paints a few words.

My last day alive. And I'm not scared.

His hand trembles. He's lying. He is very scared.

The boy with no name was here.

He lays his brush down, and looks at the moon out the window. I wonder if it has sent him dreams and beauty that way, despite the walls around him. It's clear he thinks this is the last time he'll see it.

He sits gently on his bed, and folds his hands to wait.

And then a small bluebird appears at his feet.

He looks down at her in surprise.

I am pointing Little One through the slot, and she's looking up at him quizzically. He watches as she nuzzles up to his threadbare, torn left shoe.

I don't dare to call out to him, even in a soft voice. Instead I send Little One fluttering through the air, this time leaving words behind her like a miniature blue sky-writer. *Only the witches would have you think there is more darkness in the world than there is light,* I write. *Only the witches would have you think love could ever really leave you.*

The boy shifts and pivots his head, eyes shooting to the window first. And then he looks around behind him, at the slot . . . at me.

There is the tiniest dawning of wonder on his face, mixed with the shock, as he meets my eyes. He looks just like me: dark hair, big brown eyes.

After a second, wonder is replaced by fear. His eyes dart up and down the door; he cocks his head to listen for the Time Witch. I hold my finger to my lips, heart pounding.

He slides off the bed and tiptoes to the vent, crouches down to look at me.

"Are you okay?" I ask. Which seems a silly thing to ask, in hindsight.

He blinks at me for a moment, and then shakes his head. He points to his mouth. *Is he saying he doesn't speak?* He was the loud baby, the one who got taken. And now he doesn't make a sound.

Still, I reach my hand through the slot and grab on to his. I whisper what I've dreamt of saying since the moment we set out on the whale, what seems like a lifetime ago, to save him.

"I'm your sister. I've crossed the Sea of Always to rescue you. And now I'm taking you home."

I release Wolf's hand. Little One, already inside the room, begins to grow at my command.

I turn her into a saw slicing her way silently through the door between us. My fingers tremble on my flashlight as she cuts a square quickly through the wood, and I hold it gently as it falls. The noise is barely a whisper, and the Time Witch doesn't appear.

Through the newly opened gap, Wolf studies me—and my hand nestling into his again—uncertainly.

I should be troubled by what Aria said because I know she's right. It does feel *too easy*, after all this time. But inside, I'm floating. *I am holding my brother's hand.* I tug him gently, and finally he crouches and slides through the hole into the hall, where I can finally wrap my arms around him. In my arms, he stands as stiff as wood.

"I'm sorry it took me so long," I say.

With Germ pulling my arm to get us moving, and all of us looking around like the sky is about to fall, we hurry out of the building, me holding my bag of hearts in one arm like a hostage. With the other, I am pulling Wolf behind me. His fingers feel, to me, like gold.

CHAPTER 21

We are hurrying along the road out of town, far on the outskirts where the city and houses give way to scrubby wilderness, walking as fast as we can. The sand has completely run out in my hourglass, but it doesn't matter—I have what I came for. The stars shine in the moonless sky above us. Fog blows across the land, occasionally obscuring what little we can see in the dark.

His hand is still in mine, but Wolf hasn't said a word.

Germ and Aria and I keep looking over our shoulders, knowing that any minute the witches will be after us. The

Time Witch, no doubt, has come for Wolf's years by now and found him gone. And yet here we are, untouched. I still don't understand it.

We are following the line of the sea, looking for the first sign of Chompy to show above the waves, straining our eyes for a glimpse of him.

"What about saving the world?" Germ says, keeping her voice low in the dark. "We won't stop the witches from unleashing the black hole if we don't fight them."

I don't know what to say. I never even considered that we'd get my brother without destroying the witches; I have eight hearts in my backpack, and the Time Witch still has hers. Still, all I can think of is getting Wolf to safety. Once we make it to Chompy, we can think about everything else.

Aria and I have our weapons up, and I'm growing warier as we close the distance between the city and our landing spot. The tide is out; the water has receded, making the sea farther to reach. All around us, patches of fog play hide-and-seek with the world.

We pass into the same narrow gorge between the two hills we came through earlier, which means we're getting closer to our goal. Still, its rocky walls are high, and I don't like losing sight of the sea even for a few minutes.

And then, beside me, Wolf stiffens, and begins to tremble like a leaf.

He stops walking altogether. Holding on to him, I'm jerked to a stop too.

"Wolf, we have to keep moving," I say. "We have to get you to our whale."

Wolf looks at me, his eyes wide and haunted. Something is wrong, and only he knows what. And then . . . we all see.

As the fog drifts past us, we get our first glimpses of them, shadowy blotches in the mist. They are in a circle that surrounds us, like a murder of crows.

It's strange, but as much as terror washes over me, relief washes over me too.

The moment has arrived, at last. There are no surprises. The witches are going to attack us, as we knew they would—just a little later than we planned.

The Time Witch is the only one I can make out at first, hummingbirds swirling around above her. But we are as ready as we'll ever be.

I shine Little One onto the ground and instantly grow her, her mouth enormous, hovering at my shoulder, ready to swallow in one bite the hearts of all the witches before me but one. I step forward and hoist my backpack into my hands. I open it and reach inside.

But what my hand touches is not hearts. I look down.

It's worms—a squirming, writhing tangle of worms, wriggling where our stolen treasures should be.

The hearts are gone.

CHAPTER 22

All is motionless except the fog; the last wisps of it drift inland and rise away from us into the dark hills. The clear night air reveals the rest of the witches now encircling us: Hypocriffa, the Griever, Egor, Miss Rage, Babble, Mable the Mad, the Greedy Man, Dread . . . all those we've robbed. Convenia, still, is nowhere in sight.

My mind races. How and when did they take the hearts back? My thoughts shoot to the abandoned building where we found Wolf, the tickle at my back as I knelt by Wolf's door. And suddenly I know it: the Time Witch replaced the hearts, in the moments I looked at my brother for the first time. She was toying with us, as she has from the beginning.

But before I even finish this thought, Wolf is no longer in my grasp. He's in the arms of the Time Witch instead, wrapped in her cloak. He lets out a strangled sound, like an animal. The Time Witch nestles him into one arm and holds up something silver in her other hand, dangling it back and forth and smiling at me. I reach on reflex to my wrist, and find that my bracelet and the whale whistle attached to it are gone. My heart drops to my feet.

Little One is poised above the bag of missing hearts, flapping frantically near my shoulder. The Time Witch goes on smiling, stroking Wolf's hair.

"That long walk into Salem, those nights standing in doorways in the rain, that trek through Iceland? All that time you thought you were the three of you alone, saving the world. But my dear, I knew, I waited, I watched. My birds may be thoughtless creatures, but they know how to be subtle." She looks almost gentle, the way she caresses Wolf's hair as she talks. "I could have destroyed you at any moment. I'm the *Time Witch*. As I told Dread that night by the fire—when you were spying on us from behind the rocks—playing a game against a human is like playing with puppies. It's easy. I was hoping it wouldn't be. I was hoping you would entertain me. It has been . . . disappointing."

And then she pats her sleeve, and I see a corner of the black hole blanket dangling out from where she's tucked it. Her smile deepens. "At least once the Nothing King comes, I won't need such games to feel fulfilled."

I am still in shock, still grappling with the hearts being gone, the crumbling of our plan before my eyes. All of my doubts have come true: I've made a huge mistake.

Of course she dies. They all die. That's what the Time Witch said. Who was I—Rosie Oaks—to think I could change the future?

My mind goes blank, like blacking out at a spelling bee when a crowd is watching. I look to Germ, but her eyes are closed. She pops one eye open and looks at me, trembling.

"I'm asking Chompy to help," she whispers urgently.

But Chompy couldn't rescue us even if he *could* hear Germ's ESP. We can't get out of the gorge without getting past the witches. We can't reach the water.

In another moment, on some signal I don't see, the witches move—so fast, they're a blur. They zip close around us and dart away, one after the other, as fast as light. I jerk up my flashlight but not fast enough. I feel hands flutter against me; beside me, Aria and Germ stumble left and right. We are being touched, and marked. They encircle us again, once they've finished. The whole thing has taken less than a second.

"Rosie," Aria gasps, holding her slingshot close to her doubtfully. "We need you to be extra Rosie right now and dream something up."

I blink at her. I'm trying to think of how to be something *more* than Rosie right now. Clearly I need to be *more*, but I can't imagine how. What would a *really powerful* witch hunter do? What would Aria do if her weapon could work? How would my mom fight? How fearless would Germ be? I even think of Bibi West back home. How would *she* battle us out of this if she were a hunter too?

I shine Little One onto the ground before me. I imagine her as a bomb—the most destructive thing I can think of. But as soon as she changes shape and barrels out toward the witches, the Time Witch waves a hand, and Little One's fuse burns backward . . . and then snuffs out.

I bounce the flashlight's beam along the ground, regrouping, making Little One a silver arrow a moment before I fling her at the Time Witch. She waves another hand, and the arrow slows, then turns, flying back at the three of us. Aria lets out a scream, and we all duck. It barely misses us.

I am frantic now. I make a flame, a missile, a sword, grunting as I try to send each shape pummeling toward the Time Witch, but she fends them off by barely lifting her fingers.

And then she raises her arms, as if to surrender. And out of her sleeves, the hummingbirds come. Hundreds of them pour out into the air, rising from the witch's arms like storm clouds. The other witches, on her cue, do the same.

All around us, familiars flutter and flap out of sleeves, crawl and lope from within the folds of robes. They spread into the air and across the ground toward and all around us: chameleons slithering across the dirt, magpies and hornets and bats fluttering into the air. They pin us in from all directions, coming to steal everything from us: our courage, our hope, our years. Little One flares and flickers and becomes merely her small bluebird self, chirping in terror. My imagination feels frozen shut. I simply can't get it to work.

I look to Germ for ideas, but Germ has finally abandoned her ESP, and I can see the deepening certainty in her eyes. We can't fight this. We can't even come close.

Above, the hummingbirds and bats rise high enough to block out the stars. Below them, thousands of tiny beetle feet tap across the dry ground, but it's the hyenas that reach us first, leaping out of the night toward us.

Screaming, Germ falls back under the weight of one, defenseless, but Aria holds her slingshot aloft and aims at them as they struggle. She tries to sing, but her voice cracks as it comes out. Her shot goes crooked and crazy, missing Germ and the hyena completely and slamming into a boulder that breaks apart.

"Save her!" I say to Little One. I make her a lion, the strongest, most powerful Little One I can think of, who lunges at the hyena's throat and fells it. She lunges at another that's leaping for Aria's face. She takes down three more hyenas before the bats are on us.

First it's one by one, but soon it's a torrent. I think as fast as I can, changing Little One again and again: she's a bear knocking bats from the sky, a badger devouring chameleons, a silver shield blocking the onslaught of hornets, a whip slicing at peacocks. She is brilliant, bright, changing as she fights. She is everything I try to make her.

But she is facing impossible odds.

At my side, a swarm of hornets reaches Aria, who lifts her slingshot just as they knock her over, her weapon flying out of her hands. She lunges for it. I turn Little One into a gust of wind that blows the hornets across the air. But I can see the rage they've left, all over Aria's face.

Another hyena bites me from behind, and I whip Little One toward it in the shape of a panther. The hyena goes limp as it's devoured, but I feel an aching space inside where the hyena bit me.

I'm spinning so fast, I can't even *see*, as I lash out wherever I can. I feel creatures biting me, pecking me, scratching me—and deep things inside fall away with the bites. I see it happening to Germ and Aria, too. They look confused, hopeless, enraged—all the things we can't let ourselves become. The witches are overrunning us, easily.

Aria is still trying to load her slingshot. She manages to nock a rock and howl a broken note as she unleashes it, but her shot goes crookedly careening into the dirt.

"The water! To the water!" Germ yells. But there are too many fighting against us. I'm knocked onto my back by a bloodthirsty peacock, and before I can move to get up, I'm covered by shiny brown bats. I try to make Little One a door like before, but above me, she is pulled out of the sky by hornets.

"Rosie," Aria yells, nocking another rock and letting out a scream-howl. This one clears an opening in the space between us just enough for us to see each other through the storm of creatures. "She *knew* we were at the fire that night! She was lying, *because we were listening*! This isn't where we lose. This isn't where we die!" But a growing hopelessness is taking over her face. "Rosie," she cries, "this is where we win!"

I turn my neck to see her better, but she's being devoured by curses, and despair comes over me in waves. I turn my face to the sky, the iridescent creatures swarming over me.

"This is where we win," I say in the direction of the stars, as if because Aria said it, it can be true. I see, at the edges of my vision, witches tightening a circle close around us. But instead of trying to fight, I concentrate. I remember how I used to coach myself, back before my mom remembered me. *You are the Rosie who keeps quiet,* I think as I swipe a beetle out of my mouth and clutch Little One to my chest, tears of fear squeezing out of my eyes. *You are the Rosie who makes doors in clouds. You are the Rosie who's messy, but you are the Rosie who made Little One. You are the girl who Aria and Germ and Ebb believe in.*

Peacock feathers are falling all around me as the birds nibble at my shoulders, and a witch, Dread, has come to stand over me curiously, staring down at me with his depthless gray eyes, almost pitying. I ignore him. "You are the girl who got picked last in the Farmer in the Dell, but you are the girl who got everyone to look at the sky."

I point my *Lumos* flashlight upward from my chest, grasping on to these last words in my mind. While the witches close in, they are all looking down at us. And that is why I try it.

I direct the beam up to the sky. And because it's the only thing I can think of, even though it's bizarre and even embarrassing, I send Little One shooting up toward the stars.

When she comes back down, she's not alone. Or rather, she is not just *one thing*. She shoots up into the air like a bottle rocket by herself, but when she comes down, she comes down like meteors.

The witches look up all at once to see an unexpected sight: glowing figures descending from the heavens like a swarm of octopuses.

"Are those . . . ," Dread begins to ask as I look over at Germ, who—under the weight of the familiars swarming her—is looking back at me with a dawning half-horrified, half-excited realization.

"Yes." I gasp for air as even the familiars fall away from me to gape up at the sky at thousands upon thousands of purple eight-armed aliens.

The first problem for the witches is that what they're seeing is too absurd to be real. So when the aliens begin shooting from their ray guns, the witches are too slow to move.

Fiery balls of light careen down onto the fray like rain, wiping out a swarm of bats, knocking out hordes of rabbits. Flocks of peacocks go flying into the rock walls of the gully. Throwing their arms over their heads, the witches dart for shelter, but Egor is hit and is suddenly engulfed in flames. He streaks down the gully, his robes flying behind him, until he disintegrates. Miss Rage tumbles to the ground, batting at the folds of her robe, her legs alight. The Time Witch stares at her in shock a moment before she lifts a hand to fix it, the fire reversing its course under the wiggle of her fingers, turned back in time to nothing.

The distraction leaves barely enough time for me to leap to my feet. I close the distance to Wolf at a sprint and rip him out of her arms, sending her stumbling.

But I see only too late that with impossible speed she has snatched something from me in return. My flashlight.

I hear the sickening crunch as she breaks it in two. And then, as she again lifts a hand, the aliens come to a stop in midair, and then fly backward up into the sky. Like dying fireworks, they fade into the nothingness they were before I invented them. The last glowing purple embers of them disappear into the sky.

The Time Witch grinds her foot into my flashlight, crumbling it into pieces, obliterating it.

All goes quiet.

And the time torture begins.

CHAPTER 23

I fall back, utterly defenseless, as hummingbirds engulf every inch of me. There's a sharp ache all over my body—I am being stretched like gum. But it's what's happening to my friends that scares me most.

As the birds swirl around my face, batter my eyes, my cheeks, my arms, I catch glimpses. Germ's face is getting plumper, her hair longer, her legs shorter. She's getting smaller and smaller. She looks like the Germ I knew when she was eight. Then more like Germ at five—the Germ I met in kindergarten. And then she's a baby, sitting in the sand and surrounded by hummingbirds, all reddish-blond curls, her freckles gone. She lets out a wail, tears running down her baby cheeks.

Aria's time is going forward *and* backward. She shifts into a little girl with two black braids batting the birds away, then an old woman freckled all over and curling over herself in fear, then a teenager but older than she is now.

"Rosie, what—" she cries in a creaky voice, her eyes boring into mine. And then her hair starts to turn gray; her smooth brown skin wrinkles.

Wolf's hand, which I'm clinging to despite the hummingbirds careening into us, is getting smaller. I look down at my own fingers holding his. My skin is growing creased and dry and pale. My arms are tired, wiry, and thin. My muscles ache so much, I can barely stand. The hummingbirds are taking years so fast, I am already too old to fight back.

I sink down to the ground, holding Wolf, who is now the size of a toddler, squirming in my arms. Despite all the creatures flinging themselves against me, I'm determined not to let go.

But I'm too tired, too frail. I don't have many years left to take; my time is almost gone. Aria is small again now, maybe eight or nine. Germ is crying and pounding her tiny fists on the ground.

I look at little girl Aria, who looks at me, her bottom lip quivering.

Biting down, Aria pulls her broken slingshot up high and nocks a pebble in, aiming it at the nearest witch, Dread. She lets out a half-scream, half-song cry, the deepest and most pained cry of hurt I can imagine. As she does, she shoots the rock straight at him.

There is an enormous creak, as if the sky is being torn. Several witches are knocked backward by the force. Dread, the one the rock actually *hits*, is lifted like a rag and thrown across the air. He hits the side of the gorge, and melts into iridescent gray vapor as he flies apart; gray drops of him spatter everywhere. His remains fall like rain.

The baby Germ has stopped crying. She points her hands at the rain, and laughs.

Aria and I look at each other in shock, but it's only a fraction of a moment before there is a deeper, louder sound—a kind of creaking rumble.

And then the gorge begins to shake, and its walls give way, fault lines snaking through the rock a second before it crumbles. The walls topple all around us, forcing us into the middle of the gorge as the entrances at either end collapse.

The remaining witches rise up willy-nilly from where they fell. The Time Witch takes in the view around her, and her shoulders seem to relax. Now we are outnumbered, *and* trapped. The passageway is now a pen surrounded by high walls of jagged fallen stone. Our only escape is lost—our path to the sea, gone.

I gape at my friends. Aria is a little kid. I'm at least ninety years old. Germ is a baby. Even if we were at our best, we couldn't get over that rubble. And now . . .

The hummingbirds swarm to finish us off. Young Aria scoops Germ into her arms, trying to protect her from them. I thrust Wolf's hand at her.

"Take them both! I'm too old to run!"

Aria balks for a moment, not wanting to leave me. Then she snatches Wolf's hand from mine and makes for the rubble. I watch her scramble up the mountain of broken rock, small but determined. With no strength left, I turn my back on the birds showering over me, but I keep my eyes on Aria, *willing* her and Germ and Wolf to make it up the fallen rocks for a clear run at the ocean.

And then, in horror, I see that a figure has appeared at the top of the hill above them, coming from the other side of it. She is all in purple, and she's late. But she's come just in time to cut off the escape of the people I love.

Convenia. The last witch. Behind her, a woman—silhouetted in the dusk—rises to stand, a bow arched in her hands.

My heart shudders. She draws back and shoots, an arc like a rainbow across the sky.

My eyes follow the arrow's trajectory as it flies over my head, over the thousands of hummingbirds coming to take my last breath, and straight into the heart of the witch who cast them.

The Time Witch clutches her chest, and falls into the ground. It happens so fast, you can barely see it. One moment she is there, and the next, she is swallowed into nothing. As if she never existed at all.

And beyond the ashes of hummingbirds falling from the sky, I see my mother running toward me.

CHAPTER 24

There is no celebrating, no hugging.

Instead my mom lifts me and throws me onto her back with a moan while Convenia whips baby Wolf and baby Germ into her arms so that young Aria can run free.

Already I can feel my age leaving me, the years rolling off me, my strength returning as bits of obliterated hummingbird rain down on me from the sky. But the remaining witches, screeching, terrified, enraged, are flinging everything they've got at us as we make our tripping, falling way up the rubble mountain—my mom and Convenia fighting them off the best they can.

Convenia's cats tangle with the creatures behind us, leaping into the air to snatch bats out of the sky. In the fray, one of Babble's magpies manages to peck the whale whistle from around Convenia's neck and make off with it. My mom shoots arrows behind her, but with me clinging to her back, they fly astray. Miss Rage dodges one and then another. Six witches still pursue us.

We crest the mountain and half tumble, half run down the other side. The ocean comes into view, blue and waiting and not so far away.

But it's what's missing from the ocean that stops us in our tracks.

Chompy. Chompy is nowhere to be seen. Just as I always feared, he's deserted us . . . at the moment when we need him most. And I have no whistle to call him back.

We keep running to the water's edge, and turn. Our backs to the ocean, up to our shins in the water, we face the witches coming for us. It's pandemonium as our ages twirl rapidly back to what they were. Aria, Germ, and Wolf cry out as they stretch and grow. My body burns as I get younger, stronger, taller.

We stand united but still vastly outnumbered, and now

I have no Little One to fight with. My mom shoots arrow after arrow, knocking familiars out of the sky. But she can't manage to get another witch.

"We've got to swim!" Germ says.

We all gape at her. The ocean behind us is endless. There is nowhere to go. We'd be swimming to our deaths.

"It's the only thing left to do. Chompy's coming for us. I know it! He must be rallying the whales!"

We know it isn't true. But we back into the frigid water and begin to paddle out into the sea. We have no choice.

To our shock, Convenia stays on the shore, protecting our retreat, casting her curses this way and that, her cats leaping at birds, lizards, rabbits, but she is being swamped. Finally a cloud of bats descends on her at once. From within the whirlwind, we hear her scream, and then go silent.

Breathing hard, I paddle alongside my mom, who's taken Wolf in one arm. Beside us, Germ and Aria are stroking wildly, out of breath. We are paddling into an empty frigid vista, with nothing to keep us afloat.

The witches, on the other hand, have options. They gather at the edge of the water for a moment, doing something we can't make out, and then we see their familiars all coming together—forming a fluttering writhing boat to hold them, its hull made of chameleons and scrabbling beetles, its sail made of birds and hornets. We watch in horror, helpless, as the witches climb aboard this writhing vessel and sail swiftly toward us, faster than we can swim. We paddle farther and farther, but not fast enough.

When the water begins to churn around them, we think it's only the power of wingbeats from the sail, stirring up the wind. But the foam keeps rising beneath them. The waves bubble and froth, churning foam.

"What's happening?" Aria yells.

I couldn't say. It's a familiar sight, but I can't think why.

And then I realize it's the kind of splash Chompy makes when he rises. Only, it is everywhere, all around us.

The whales all breach the surface of the sea at once. Eleven of them rise from the ocean, swamping the creature boat in waves, sending familiars scattering into the water, where the whales devour them like krill. The whales snatch scores of them in their powerful jaws before plummeting back underwater. And as they do, what's left of the boat capsizes, and all of its inhabitants—six stunned witches—tumble into the sea.

The surface of the water whips and swirls as they disappear under the waves, creating a swirling whirlpool beneath us that we fear will suck us in. But then we feel a smooth surface rising up underneath us. Chompy lifts us above the water, fighting against the current to swim us away from it.

A few more giant ocean bubbles burble and pop. And then, the whirlpool disintegrates. The sea goes quiet.

We're all silent for several moments, disbelieving, trying to catch our breath, as the waves roll in and out and swoosh against the shore.

The witches have drowned in the same sea that carried them through time.

Gasping, we slide off Chompy's back and paddle with the last of our strength for the shore, where we throw ourselves onto the sand and stare out at the water, in shock.

"What just happened?" Aria breathes as we all watch the ocean, which is still and calm.

"Chompy loves me," Germ says. "He wanted to help."

I blink at her, trying to take it in. Does Chompy really love Germ like Germ loves Chompy? I blink at her, panting, feeling foolish. I always thought Germ's loving everything and everyone no matter what was her weakness. Instead it rallied the whales . . . and I guess, possibly, saved the world. I guess Germ's witch hunting weapon is love.

The sun is rising. And we watch it, in awe.

"The tide's coming in," Aria says. But none of us bothers to move.

My mother is holding on to Wolf with both hands as the waves lap at our legs. I lean against her arm, and the three of us hold each other tight. There are so many questions I want to ask. But Wolf beats me to it with one of his own.

He is staring at the woman who won't let go of him. And then he looks at me, questioning.

I can tell he wants to ask who this woman is who's holding on to him for dear life. But whether he has no voice, or simply can't bring himself to use it yet, I don't know.

"That's our mom," I say with a smile. "She's a witch hunter like us."

I say it without thinking it through. But it feels like a sudden release, like a breath of comfort, like *rest*.

For so long I thought I was the only witch hunter, and then—even after Aria came, I thought I had to do it mostly alone. But I was wrong.

And not just because my mom has arrived and gotten back her power. But because Germ called the whales with her love and they saved us, and Aria, even with her broken songs, kept us from harm. And Wolf has the sight . . . and who knows what gifts to go with it? And people, just by doing little things, leave moonlight where they walk.

We are so different in the ways that we fight—and we are so small in the face of the dark—but we are, none of us, alone.

And then Chompy rises, resurfacing. He opens his mouth to allow us in, waiting.

Wolf cringes back, afraid.

Already Germ is standing and retracing our steps, throwing each and every whale whistle she can find, left behind from the witches, angrily into the sea.

The whales will never answer to us or anyone else again, unless it's by choice.

It will take Wolf time to learn he is safe. It will take time for me, too. I know I will need to reassure him about so many things.

"It's okay, Wolf. I think he wants to take us home," I say. "Are you ready?"

Off the coast of San Francisco, on an evening in 1855, it is high tide.

The waves lap at what's been left behind. Familiars that haven't flown and crawled and loped away to return their stolen quarry to the world have disintegrated on the beach, and their ashes have been slowly swept away by the waves. Shells tumble in the lapping water, as do shreds of colored cloaks, and a broken tin box that once belonged to a witch who had a seed of mercy planted in her heart. A pink glow is fading around it, as if its contents might not have disintegrated like the rest. As if what it held might have moved on to somewhere pink and sparkling instead.

A limp black blanket, recently completed, easy to mistake for a cloak or a rag, lies upon the shore, its edges fluttering as the waves lap farther and farther up the beach to claim it. Finally it is washed into the sea. Pulled out into the deep, it flutters open in the water, spreads like a flower or a blob of ink.

The blanket, as empty as emptiness can be, is pulled into the currents. It's so full of darkness, it almost turns the corner into light. Its depths are endless.

And out of this blanket something seemingly small and insignificant flutters down toward the ocean floor, something from another side of the universe.

A crow feather, but not the usual beautiful color of a crow. This feather is the color of a void.

It spins and churns as it descends.

And as it falls, it grows.

CHAPTER 25

We are swimming across the Sea of Always and—though we are hundreds of years and three thousand miles from home—we do not have far to go.

We are on the shag rug in the main room, where we're gathered in a circle, sitting together in silence. I think the people around me are all trying to imagine what a world without witches means. But all I can think of is Little One.

My mom has Wolf wrapped in a blanket and in her arms, as if she can make up for all the time she did not get to baby him, by never letting him go. He hasn't spoken since we left the shore.

He's a quiet boy after all, silent in fact, and a mystery. It'll take a long time to get to know him. We're the family who's loved him for years, but we're also strangers—people he never expected to exist. And it will take months, maybe years, to prove to him how much we'd give to make him safe.

But also, it's like I always thought between us. He has my eyes and my smallness. We both scratch our nose in the same way. I suspect he feels it too, that we know each other in our bones.

And I know that soon, we'll tell him his history. But for now, we take our time.

In the corner, Ebb is the faintest wisp of a flicker of a ghost, but he's also still here. As soon as we've dropped Aria off, we will head back home to Seaport, and back to the safety of his grave. He'll recharge—we hope—to the bright and glowing ghost he was before the Time Witch stole him. We just have to make it that far, and I know that we will.

The question is, what kind of world are we returning to? What will it be like to rise to a place where everything witches have stolen has been returned? Some things are beyond even my imagining.

"Where are we headed?" I ask Aria finally. She's been at the front of the ship giving Chompy his orders. "Where and when is your never-ending day with your sister going to take place?"

Aria smiles sadly, and shakes her head.

"It's not," she says.

"What do you mean?" Germ asks as we all look at her sharply.

"I don't want to go back in time and pretend Clara isn't going to leave," Aria says. "And I don't want to stay in one place forever, even if it's a happy one. It wouldn't be enough after all I've seen of the world, and witches, and you guys. . . ." She frowns, uncomfortable with being so mushy. "I don't need to hold on to Clara forever, pretending she's not the person who leaves me. I need to let her go. Really, I need to let being *mad* at her go. I want to stop holding on so tight to the *wrong* of it. Even if I still don't know how."

"Maybe it's like, forgiving someone is a gift you give yourself," Germ says quietly. Germ, as smushy-hearted as she is, finds forgiving as easy as breathing. The rest of us have to work at it.

Aria nods at her, and looks at Ebb. "I asked Chompy to head to May 4, 1934. The day before you died, Ebb. I'm giving you the voucher."

Ebb's glow flares up so suddenly and brightly, I worry he might go out altogether.

"I know," Aria goes on, "there are two people there you really want to see."

We arrive at the backyard of the only house on Waterside Road in 1934—*my* house, long before it was destroyed by the Memory Thief—on a clear, fully moonlit night. I'm so excited to see the full moon in its glory, I could hug it if I could reach that far.

We climb, one by one, out of Chompy's mouth, step ankle-deep into the water, and walk up onto the beach. Familiar ghosts wander around on the sand, barely noticing us, ghosts that I've been seeing on and around this property ever since I got the sight.

We step onto dry land near the cave where Ebb was caught by the tide the day he died. And where he showed me my mother's weapon, back when I vowed I would only ever hunt one witch.

The moment we are on solid ground, all our hopes come true. Ebb begins to charge up like a light bulb. He glows bright and luminous and fully ghostly again, as easy as that. He is home.

He looks up, as if to smile at the Moon Goddess. We

all do. The moon sits in the sky with its ladder dangling as if nothing has happened at all.

I have the sense, which has been with me ever since I got the sight, that everywhere the world is speaking—crickets telling each other "I'm here," owls grumbling as the darkness wakes them from their long day's slumber.

The Beyond sparkles above it all, serene, mysterious, full of the unknowable—not the silver glow of moonlight and hope, but the pink sparkle of something even better. Gazing up at it, we suddenly hear voices, laughter. Up on the hill we see a boy doing something with his dad. He does not see us, of course. This version of Ebb—the living one—doesn't have the sight.

I hear his dad call out to him. *Robert.*

Ebb stares up at the cliff, his eyes wide, his glowing face flickering and flushed. His parents are there—not waiting for him, but there for him to haunt for one never-ending, happy day of his living childhood. To watch over. To be close.

He looks at me. I put my hand toward his, though we can't touch. I look back at Chompy's wide-open mouth, waiting for us even without the whistle to call him.

Above, the sky is darkening, the stars seeming to blink out one by one—though there are only a few small clouds in the sky. I register it, but only vaguely. It's strange but unimportant. I'm too sad about letting Ebb go. I feel like a part of me is tearing away.

I watch our hands, mine a little smaller than his, so close to each other but unable to touch. I wish I could have known Ebb when he was alive. I wish, for just once, we could hug.

I know the moment can't last forever, so finally I let my hand fall. It's then that we feel the breeze kick up. We all look out at the water, at a dark patch—now definite, circular, and widening—growing in the sky above the sea. It reminds me of an ink blot spreading, creating a shadow on the water below.

"What *is* that?" Aria says. But none of us can answer. It's a moment when things go from predictable to strange . . . a sudden pivot into fear.

In the distance, we see ghosts pointing at the vast expanse overhead. Above, clouds and cloud shepherds are being whipped across the sky as if by a hurricane-force wind, then sucked upward toward the widening dark. Beneath us, the ground begins to shake.

We gape for a moment in shock as the emptiness in the sky spreads. Even the living Ebb on the hill and his dad stare above in wonder. Behind them, someone is shouting to them urgently to come inside. This is something *everyone* can see, living and dead. Down the beach, the ghosts begin to scream.

"A hole?" Germ says, her voice wooden in fear. "Is that a black hole?"

At the moment she says it, I feel it's the truth.

The Time Witch, her blanket. She left it behind. There's no time to reason it out or try to understand.

"Let's go," my mom says flatly, jumping into action. She grabs my hand and Wolf's and pulls us toward the water where Chompy waits; she nods to Germ and Aria to follow. I look back at Ebb, a question on my face that I can't put into words.

We trail along behind my mom, stumbling toward Chompy on instinct, knowing we need to hide . . . that the whole *world* needs to. I look back again with relief to find Ebb hurrying along behind me, the last of the group. He's following, but he keeps looking back at the boy on the hill in the arms of his dad—gaping at the sky.

We climb into Chompy's mouth, stumbling over ourselves; even Chompy is shaking and eager to move. Glowing and wincing, Ebb leaps on board behind us, whooshing between the whale's jaws as they close. There's a vicious rocking as Chompy turns course, and we all fall

all over the room—which goes topsy-turvy as he tilts and dives toward deeper water, hurtling into the sea and down, down, down as fast as he can go. Getting her footing by grabbing a wall, Aria runs into our bedroom and emerges with her snow globe. She cradles it in her hands, keeping it safe just in time, because Chompy now turns so steeply downward that we all roll along the floor, and then become plastered to the wall.

The numbers on the monitor spin. We can hear water gurgle and churn beyond Chompy's walls as he dives deeper and deeper, as fast as a bullet. Around us, lights begin to flicker.

"He's not supposed to go so deep," Ebb says. "He'll break."

"I know, I know," I gasp. But what are we supposed to do? Where can anyone hide from a black hole? Even the Sea of Always and all it contains will be swallowed up.

We go deeper, and deeper, and then suddenly Chompy stops. The whale shudders. And the lights on board flicker and go out.

"We can't go any farther down," Ebb says. "That's it."

We sit, touching each other's hands in the dark. All we can do is wait.

Around us, we hear the heavy sound of far-off crashes,

thuds. Is it cliffs crashing into the sea? Mountains crumbling, cities toppling? The whole world ending at once? My mind flies to the things and people we love up there. The living Ebb and his parents, Germ's mom, Bibi West, D'quan Daniels, the ghosts in my house, the store clerk in town, all the people everywhere, animals, bugs, stop signs, people, buses, trees, cities. Our beautiful living breathing Earth.

Chompy lets out a long slow whale call—crying out for the other whales, calling to anything that might be out there. But the sea is silent.

We blink at each other without seeing each other in the dark. We are quiet for a long time, waiting for whatever is coming. There is nothing else to do.

And then I notice the tiniest hint of a light, coming from Aria's lap.

"It's my snow globe," Aria says after a moment. The tiny light has come on in the little house. She caresses the globe gently with her hands.

"It looks so safe in there," Germ says wistfully, as if longing to curl up inside it. "I wish we could hide in *there*."

We stare at it for a long time.

"A tempest in a teacup," Aria whispers. She looks up at me. Something is connecting in her eyes. They have a sudden twinkle of recognition in them, but I don't know what it means.

"The Time Witch," she says. "Her trinkets. Her gambles. Voices from a mouse hole. A forest in a sock." She takes a deep breath and lets it out. "Clara." She rubs her hand along the glass. "The Brightweaver said time and space are entwined and bendable. What if they are bent . . . in here?"

She cups the snow globe lovingly. "Clara would know. But it's the end of the world, and I won't see her again. Oh, Clara," she whispers. "I love you."

And then she begins to sing. A song that sounds like what losing someone is. She sings *sadness*, the kind of sadness you feel when you forgive and finally let go.

A thread of light trails out of Aria's mouth, like we saw in Iceland. Colorful, like the rainbow mist that flies behind my mom's arrows and the luminous light that makes—*made*—my precious Little One glow. It is purple and pink and beautiful, and it moves like a ribbon slowly through the air, wrapping itself around Aria's hands and the snow globe inside them.

And then it does something strange.

It threads right through the glass into the snow globe, and reaches the tiny door of the house with the light on.

Inside Chompy, you could hear a pin drop.

The tiny thread of Aria's song wraps around the tiny knob of the door and pulls it open. And then . . . five very tiny figures come swimming out, unmistakably human, each the size of a pinky nail. That's when Aria's hands jerk in surprise, and she drops the globe.

In the dark, we hear it shatter.

The tiniest light from the globe is lost. And the despair around us is complete.

And then, in the blackness, we hear murmuring in the middle of the room.

"Ugh, I think I cut myself," a gruff voice says.

"Oh, get a Band-Aid, you'll be fine," says another, annoyed.

"Still clumsy," another voice says, and this one makes Aria gasp.

Only Germ thinks to find where the scented candles have fallen, and light a match.

In the glow, five new people sit facing us: a woman with pink freckled cheeks and a peg leg; a man with a white beard and glasses; two black-haired boys who look almost the same age; and a teenage girl who looks a lot like Aria, with one puff of a bun above her head, wearing a hot-pink hoodie. I know it's Clara, without even having to ask.

"What did we miss?" she asks, smiling at Aria, before her sister falls on her with a scream.

As soon as Aria stops squeezing her neck, it rushes out of Clara, how one night while Aria slept, Clara found her way into the snow globe—where she suspected other witch hunters might have been trapped by the Time Witch. How she found them . . . but then found herself trapped too. How she's been hoping Aria would save them all ever since.

The two sisters sit back, wiping away ecstatic tears. Clara says she has a lot to be sorry for, but clearly sees by our faces that now is not the time to go over it.

"Okay, but seriously." She looks around the room as she turns solemn and nervous, as Germ lights the only candle that hasn't shattered. "You all look *bad*. What did we miss? Where are we? How *are* things?"

We all look at each other in the flickering light.

"Well," Germ blurts out, "it's nice to finally meet you. I'm Germ. I like my iguana, Eliot Falkor; shows about pet psychics; and my boyfriend, D'quan, who might think I'm dead and also might be doomed. Also"—she clears her throat, glancing around the room at the rest of us—"the Nothing King has unleashed chaos, and the world is about to be swallowed by a black hole." She takes a breath. "We're mostly sure the earth is pretty much destroyed. We might be all that's left of it because we're at the deepest part of the Sea of Always. But it can't be long before the black hole devours us, too." She leans back, out of breath. "So . . . things are . . . not great."

The newcomers look at each other in silence.

"Well," the woman with the peg leg says after a moment, standing and brushing glass off her legs and sighing. "Sounds like we're in a bit of a pickle. I guess we'd better get going."

"Going where?" I ask, looking around. We're trapped in a whale at the bottom of the sea on a doomed planet.

"You don't spend endless years stuck inside a witch's snow globe without learning a thing or two about space and time," the woman says.

She scans the room, noticing the magazine crumbled by our La-Z-Boy.

"Oh, this'll do nicely," she says, staring at the photo on the cover. It's *Pet Psychi*c magazine, *The Outer Space Issue*. There's a picture of the swirling Milky Way on the front with an inset of a thoughtful-looking Labradoodle in the upper right-hand corner. The headline reads: CAN YOUR PET CONTROL DISTANT PLANETS WITH ITS MIND?

She traces a circle around the Milky Way photo with

her finger. One moment the picture is just a picture. The next, the Milky Way sparkles with motion and light, like the waterfall painting I saw.

The woman slips a fingernail under the circle she's traced, and tugs. It opens, like a door, and there are stars swirling beyond its small opening.

"Prepare yourself. Things are about to get a little weird."

We—my mother, my brother, Aria, Germ, Ebb, and I—stare at her like she has to be joking. Things are *about to* get weird?

Little One is gone. The moon and its goddess are probably gone too. The cloud shepherds have been sucked into a void of nothingness. And we are being summoned into a piece of paper by what I can only assume is the League of Witch Hunters in the flesh. Looking around at them, they are kind of a lopsided lot—disheveled, not necessarily warrior-like.

Immediately I like this about them. If I'm honest, it feels just about right.

The doorway on the magazine keeps growing, growing, growing until it is big enough to at least stick a hand into.

I reach for my flashlight but remember it's gone too. How climbing into such a place will help us save the world from a black hole and the Nothing King, I don't know. But by now, I guess anything is possible.

Our group climbs into the hole, one by one, feet first. Despite the fact that the doorway is about the size of a fist, once each person gets a few toes in, they manage to get the rest of themselves in too, and then shimmy down inside. I'm reluctant to let Wolf and my mom out of my sight, and I tug on Wolf's shirt as he goes to step in. But my mom shakes her head to reassure me she's got him. Finally I am a kid, and my mom is leading the way. I let him go.

It looks like it must be painful.

Germ, because she's always so brave, goes before me. She shrinks to the size of the hole bit by bit as she enters it. And then the woman with the peg leg, bringing up the rear, nods to encourage me to follow.

What I am stepping into is anybody's guess.

But I am with my friends—my weird, broken, strange, wild, lopsided friends. Perfectly imperfect. Not a *lot of friends*, but the right ones.

I take the hand Germ reaches back to me, and follow her toward whatever waits.

ACKNOWLEDGMENTS

Thank you to Kristin Gilson and Liesa Abrams for shepherding this story and lighting the way. Thank you to my agent, Rosemary Stimola, for all of the sharing, wisdom, and support. I'm so grateful to Kirbi Fagan and Heather Palisi for the beautiful cover, Bara MacNeill for her awe-inspiring attention to detail, and Chelsea Morgan for their guidance.

I could not have written through a pandemic year if it were not for Tina Mueller and her family: our bond has been the great gift of a challenging time. Thank you to Robyn for always being my trusted reader, friend, and style consultant. Thank you to Mark for being my incredible partner and love. And thank you finally to my mom, who read to me and with me, who kept all my books on her shelf and sent them to her friends, and who always let me be my dreamy and woods-wandering self. I miss her more than words can say.

ABOUT THE AUTHOR

Jodi Lynn Anderson is the bestselling author of several critically acclaimed books for young people, including the May Bird trilogy and *My Diary from the Edge of the World*, a *Publishers Weekly* Best Book of 2015. Jodi holds an MFA in Writing and Literature from Bennington College. She lives with her husband, two children, a dog who takes everything too far, and two hermit crabs.